I0524571

STILL LIFE
WITH ALLEN KEYS

—

BRIEN COLE

ETT IMPRINT, SYDNEY

Exile Bay

This edition published by ETT Imprint, Exile Bay 2018

This book is copyright. Apart from any fair dealing for the purposes of private study, research, criticism or review, as permitted under the Copyright Act, no part may be reproduced by any process without written permission. Inquiries should be addressed to the publishers:

ETT IMPRINT
PO Box R1906
Royal Exchange NSW 1225
Australia

Copyright © Brien Cole 2018

ISBN 978-1-925706-06-2 (ebook)
ISBN 978-1-925706-07-9 (paper)

Design by Hanna Gotlieb

CONTENTS

What's wrong with the rudder?
The boat goes in circles
And not one gull.

—

George Seferis

STILL LIFE WITH ALLEN KEYS

An Introduction

1. Sarah Roth answers the phone

Sarah Roth took a phone call from her distressed daughter.

Sarah Roth as always took seven long calm breaths before she said' "Tell me about it."

And so, Diana began the story; Diana, her "Botticelli Angel", the beautiful one, bundles of tasselled strawberry blond hair, fine boned alabaster skin, eleven freckles across her forehead, startling doe deer eyes and an equally animated smile, who dresses with a flair, a flick, and a folly. Diana, the difficult one, the one ruled by the squalls of emotion. Diana, her youngest daughter, began her story, but not from the beginning, rather from the beginning of the moment where she had last left off, last telephone call, as though it was a sequence, in a long line of episodes, which in essence it is. (But also, a beginning which would make no sense to us, we need a truer beginning.)

If we were to ask Diana, where she would start this story, she would answer; the day she first licked the colour of strawberry ice-cream at Eastern Beach. If we asked Sarah, where she would start the story, she would choose; the day she finally succumbed to the masculine charms of Luke Beveridge. And if you asked Allen Keys where he would start the story; he would choose the day he first meet Sarah Roth, again on Eastern Beach, by arrangement over email, for theirs was a modern relationship. A soft sunlight day, where the high clouds leant the daylight a water colour opaqueness, pond green waters on which red rust freighters weigh, while Sarah waits on the concrete steps under the palms. Sarah in yellow dress with red embroidered flowers and a red ribbon flowing from a pale straw hat. She has dark hair, tightly curled, small, petite, with the olive skin of the Levant, she is not a Fairhaven person, or at least not the Fairhaven that Allen grew up in. She is a fire-cracker, a Catherine wheel, a hissing, fizzing, fuse, with the same fine face as her daughter. Sarah Roth is beautiful. But we are not going to start there either, we are going to start with Sarah's lists.

2. A Cow Girl has her Reasons

Sarah Roth had five good reasons for being with Allen Keys and only one of them was the sheer appropriateness of his name.

The reasons in order are;

1. He is handsome enough, not "Oh my God!" handsome, not fabulously model handsome but handsome enough, and Sarah Roth is a very attractive woman.
2. He is a decent enough, (sometimes reason number two moves into the same position under reasons not to be with Allen Keys) decent means loyal, it means mostly considerate and more moral than not, (it also means, some of the loyalty is about trepidation, being simply too scared to grab life by the short and curly's.)
3. He makes things, this could be reason one except for Sarah Roth's vanity. Her father made things, she deeply appreciates the making of things. Sarah Roth herself, is a Cow Girl, Allen Keys a Repairman, that at least is their joke, Sara is a research scientist at CSIRO Belmont, specializing in Bovine pathology. while Allen is a repairman, or eclectic amateur engineer and inventor, if you want to up-market him and Sarah sometimes does.
4. They had lived up until the day that they'd met, parallel and equally oddball lives. They are both oddballs, reason enough in itself.
5. The fifth reason sounds the simplest, but it isn't, it just so much isn't. It's because their children get on, mostly.

Allen Keys is not a list person, the only lists he ever writes look like this

1. four by two, Malibu, two metres, ten of.
2. 50 mm brass screws, Phillips head.
3. 500 ml wood glue, clear.
    And are written on scraps of paper in his workshop. But if he did write such a list, it would look something like this;
    *   He had already dreamt of her, years before he met her and many, many times.

* She is very beautiful, although beautiful is probably the wrong word for people their age, handsome perhaps.

* No one believes they should be together, and he likes to surprise people, that's not a good reason but the reason beneath it is, Allen Keys likes that's she's smart, and funny and quirky, and just mad enough, even if this smattering of reasons has not ended up well up till now.

* They have lead parallel lives; they have been to the same places, read the same books, listened to the same music, raged against the same things.

* She is Jewish, just like his grandmother (on his mother's side).

Sarah knew people found them a curious mix, she knew her friends were initially concerned about her lowly status, his inability to earn money, neither of which worried Sarah and both of which were exaggerations. It wasn't that which worried Sarah, and it wasn't his propensity to disappear into a project, she was quite capable of doing that herself, rather that people where uncomfortable around them. There is a look, a slightly con-descending look which says, "I would have thought you could have done better." They mean after Luke, Luke Beveridge, senior scientist, head of department, and ex-husband. She knew that Allen Keys was as far from Luke as she could run and nobody was surprised that she went there, only that she stayed.

What they didn't know, what the couldn't know, what they didn't have a right to know, is that she'd never felt herself with Luke rather she always felt she was an extension of him. She feels herself more often with Allen probably because he doesn't take so much space. She has room to expand.

3. Back to the Phone Call

Diana is in crisis, again, her emotional gyroscope has gone haywire, because, "you know how I fell in love with Oakley, and that was so hard because Oakley is a girl and that means I must be a lesbian, and how I struggled with that. You know how I really didn't want to be a lesbian, but Oakley's such a great person, but how I've always liked boys before. You know I've always liked boys, so how could I be a lesbian. And maybe Oakley isn't a lesbian because she has had boyfriends too. Well you know all that. And you know how I've got to do right by Lockie (her son, she always has to do right by Lockie, but doing right by Lockie always means Diana does exactly what Diana wants since that must be what Lockie wants too, LOL) You know, well maybe I'm not as lesbian as I thought, you'd like that huh. I'm sort of really into my Yoga teacher, he's really cool and has this wisdom that I can really get into and he's older than me and Lockie would really like a man kind of thing. You know all of that, well, I don't know what to do. And I sort of need you guys to look after Lockie while me and Oakley work this shit out. And you know how much Lockie loves Allen, and Allen loves Lockie. You know!"

4. Allen Keys Workshop

Allen adores Lockie.

Allen Keys is making something; something weird, something grand, something new. He is making it for and with Lockie, it is their "thing-a-me-jig". It makes noise, a lot of noise.

Allen Keys has a library of Popular Mechanic magazines he has collected from the Saint Vincent DePaul opportunity shops most of his life, random issues from random years.

September, 1953, the year of his birth,

March, 1974, the year he met Francis,

June, 1983, the year of Sam's birth,

July, 1985, the year he divorced Francis,

December, 1999 the year he met Sarah.

A tattered library along the ledge above his work bench, torn, moldy and dusty. They are in chronological order but far from complete. He doesn't care. He rarely looks at them. Not until this project, not until he needed the circuit diagram for the single note "A". December, 1972, the Whitlam government is elected and Allen Keys escapes conscription.

Circuit diagram for the Key of "C". And so, it began, the transformation of Lockie's light switch into something so much grander.

Sarah sat on a stool in the workshop watching All solder.

"Who knows how to solder anymore?"

"Sam does. His grandfather taught him."

Allen Keys is a quiet man who likes to tinker more than talk, likes to find a way to solve problems others leave alone. He is inventive, clever and can see a problem in a way that no one else can, this has both kept him employed and lost him employment over the years. He is also very skilled, but this is the Allen Keys other people rarely see. He is happiest in his workshop, and Sarah has long ago worked out that this is the place to talk to All, but only so long as it is a tinkering project, not a big, difficult, consuming project. This is a tinkering project.

"We have to talk about Diana."

Yes, they have to talk about Diana. They talk a lot about Diana, Diana has dominated their conversations for years. As Sam did once and Melissa never has. Beautiful Diana with her tumbling mass of strawberry blond hair, small, energetic mercurial, his "Botticelli Angel", their troubled daughter. Or more correctly Sarah and Luke's troubled daughter. They talk about Diana, they bail-out Diana, but neither of them are certain it has done her any good. No, they know it hasn't but they have to do something, they are parents. And they will do everything they can do to rescue Diana from herself. As they once rescued Sam, but have never rescued Melissa.

5. Sam exits stage right, enters stage left

Sam ran away from his mum. Sam moved in. A sullen, unco-operative, teenage boy, he came with one case of clothes and a skate-board, driven in a van by Max, Francis's now long-term partner. He'd never owned much, a minimal change of clothes, either brown or green, his skateboard and a record turntable. Sam doesn't like things he can't pull apart and re-assemble, which meant he also had a screwdriver, a pair of long neck pliers, a pair of circuit pliers, and his grandfather's flight computer. All of which he moved into his room and didn't come out. No, he condescended to eat at the dining room table, but did so unpleasantly and professed vegetarianism, he would have been a vegan if he'd known it was an option. He'd taken his grandfather's death hard.

Allen knew that, what he didn't know was how to draw his son back into the world. And for once Sarah hadn't an answer either.

Allen guessed part of the answer was his grandfather. Allen Key's ex-father-in-law, Air Commodore Elliot Pullman OBE, Francis's father, Sam's grandfather, Lockie's great grandfather by common law marriage. After Allen divorced Sam's mother, Allen rather than Francis would bring Sam to see his grandparents. Elliot loved Sam, so much so that he was able to forgive Allen almost everything; and accept that maybe it wasn't solely Allen's fault. Allen walked back into their house after the ten years of exclusion, after ten years of being told he had no right to be there, carrying Sam. Nothing was said, Elliot invited Sam and Allen into his garage to get to know them both, men to men, soldering electronic circuits boards, always electronic circuit boards. And suddenly they were mates, Elliot no longer the "Air Commodore" just three blokes in a shed. Sam perched on a stool fiddling with valves and pliers, four years old and excited.

He made Sam a radio in an old cigar box, AM only, but Sam didn't care, he could run through the dials of crackle and song. Even now Sam cannot hear radio crackle without thinking of him; thinking of wires, thinking of valves, thinking of cathodes and circuits and dials, thinking of stories of a long-ago life. Building a radio from parts they could scrounge on the island of Luzon behind Japanese lines, flying into Singapore in an old DC3, through Himalayan thunderstorms, crackling light, and before they could see it, the light on the shore, they smelt cloves and cinnamon, smoke, shit and spice. That was the year Francis was nine, and where was her father, fighting a war, not even the last war, just the one before that in the jungles of Asia, again and again.

Allen invited Sam into the shed, gave him a bench and his own set of tools, it won't be like grandpa, but it's the best he can do. Of course, he should have known it, it wasn't enough.

In the end, it was Diana who rescued his son, with her exuberant energy and an old Malibu surfboard, she took the boy surfing on the beach near the bluff. Surfing was something a boy could live for. Sam was still sullen, unresponsive and dour but at least there is a spark, at the turn of the tide, when the breeze is running off-shore and the swell is just right. Diana didn't stay surfing for long, she stayed about as long as she did anything, which ended the bickering about the use of the board. It's the wrong board however, in that harsh teenage voice. The right board was something he'd make for himself, and even more strangely, he'd make it in wood.

"I want to hang ten on a parquetry floor."

They could do it together and it changed both their lives. Sam sold the second board he made to one of his friends, the third to a life guard, the forth to a guy he met on the beach. Allen's not sure, how many he is up to now.

"Sam should talk to Diana, they are close."

He should, he agreed, but he's not sure he would.

"What talk to my sister about her dam dyke!"

6. Getting there.

Allen drove the old Peugeot fast. North along Mount Duneed Road, through the Barrabool Hills, skirting Geelong, Sarah sits in the passenger seat her feet on the dash, watching from the windows the familiar countryside, familiar now, since she has known Allen, but more familiar to Allen. Catching glimpses of estuary and ocean and all it's many blues, ultramarine, cobalt, Prussian, pastel, while Allen, she knows will be thinking of the hills, the valleys, the river and lakes. Allen's father, the science teacher, had a passion for geology, for it's treasures, the gemstones and gold, for it's knowledge, the fossils and strata, but mostly for forces which formed it, the volcanic history of Western Victoria. Sarah is whistling the aria from the "Pearl Fishers," as the road slowly climbs higher into the hill country. Sleeping dogs on hill towns roads, miner's cottages, forest shade on low cloud mist the wipers slap, the rich red loam of volcanic soils, the rich red smell of fungal damp, and the tang of eucalyptus, flip, flop, flip, flop, the wipers smudging ocean salt, and summer dust of coastal towns, as they enter the verandah'd streets of the old gold town Buffalo Springs.

It's an old house in an old town, a town whose fortune has risen and fallen and risen and fallen and risen again, and not for the first time, and not for the last, Allen contemplates the geomorphology of towns and lives, the laying down of sediment, the houses built of booms which fall to disrepair, and new buildings of the next great boom. Buffalo Springs never quite boomed enough to lose its gold rush splendour, it boomed again in the twenties but slumbered through the great urban ugliness of the post war years, fortunately, architecturally at least.

7. Anne Bloody Oakley

It is an old house, an old miner's cottage on a thickly wooded hill above the Buffalo Springs Lake, where Allen loves to hire the rowboats. Miranda is here, she had come up the night before and her and Diana are both vaguely hungover. Anne "Oakley" Somerton, Diana's partner, a fey girl with a phoenix tattooed on her left arm and "pull" tattooed on her left trigger finger. She has short bristled hair, she is taller than Diana, tanned, and despite her butch appearance has a gentle, wistful face. They have only met her once before and only them briefly. Diana worried what they would think, Diana worried what they would feel. Sarah thinks, little of the girl, and a lot of the situation, which she had already concluded was another Diana disaster. Allen thinks little of the situation and feels a great deal about the girl. He adores her, as does Lockie, she is loads of fun.

Oakley, she is always Oakley, has been since she'd first held a gun in her hand, at the edge of the Menindee Lakes, shooting beer cans off an old Mallee stump. An outback girl from the Great Anna Branch of the Darling River, she grew up on a ten-thousand-acre sheep station straddling one of the lessor lakes. She likes to play it up, just a bit, the outback girl, but it is also the very core of her being, who she is. Diana had dreaded telling All about Oak, he can be so conservative sometimes. The moment they met Oakley simply tipped her Akubra in his comic direction and said, "Yep."

"Yep," Yep, you'll do as if it was her and not his judgement which was important and All agreed, "Yep", she'll do. Bizarre!

All, Oakley and Lockie will go down to the lake, and let the girls talk, but later, after lunch later, because Sarah is Jewish, and Jewish families eat.

They ate vegetarian Lasagna, polenta chips and salad, a bottle of Mount Duneed Pinot Noir. Lockie, on his Lockie chair is playing with his food, fiddling with his lasagna but eating his chips. They are all a little tense. Diana and Miranda exchanging sister glances, and Oakley looking glum. Sarah trying to keep things cordial, keep things light, keep things together enough. Allen is between Lockie and Oakley, he is helping Lockie eat the lasagna and trying to engage a distracted Oakley. Allen neither knows what to do or what to think about what is happening, or what is threatening here, although nothing is actually happening here right now, they are having lunch, but threatening, oh threatening, towering, turbulence, tornados and great lightening flash, this is like Elliot in the old DC3, smelling the landfall, he cannot yet see, and praying like hell that they make it through to Changi.

Allen Keys doesn't want it to be like this, but can't see how it could ever be otherwise, you need a different kind of toughness to be with Diana, the toughness to ride the emotional storms, or maybe, just maybe, he ponders, you need a kind of callousness, a kind of indifference to Diana's whims. You need to keep Diana slightly off-keel, you need to keep her from being bored, and Oakley, the tattooed, spiky, gun totting Oakley is just too damn predictable. And as much as Allen hadn't wanted Diana to end up partnered with a girl, that was a girl in theory and not this girl. They'd thought she might have stayed with Lockie's father, the Afghan, Mohamed, heir to the noble race of cameleers, except he wasn't, nor was he an Australian, he neither had a residence permit nor a legitimate visa, God knows where she found him from, yet Diana has one great talent, finding people. They have been trying for some time now to get Mohamed permission to return to Australia, it is difficult, it is bordering on impossible, and Diana has been distracted.

8. The Boat House of Dreams

After lunch Allen took Lockie and Oakley down to the lake, "To hire a pirate ship, won't we, won't we!"

"Yes, we will Lockie."

A bird chirping, early afternoon, late summer walk, peppermint gums, dried grass and dust, a long walk through the trees to the lake and the boat house, Lockie running ahead. When Allen was a little older than Lockie, he'd wanted to own the boat house, to rent out row boats on the lake, to be a ferryman taking passengers to the island, to spend his life just mucking around with boats, today he will be Lockie's ferryman, "second lieutenant" Lockie is "captain", Oakley is "first Lieutenant", it's only right.

He feels for Oakley. People leave people, he knows that; Francis left him, Luke left Sarah, sometimes for good reasons, sometimes not. Allen Keys doesn't have anything he can say to Oak to make this better, Sarah might have, she is better at this which is why she is with Diana. Oakley is sad, she is losing something, she is doubly losing, both Diana and Lockie. Allen has been the reciprocate of Diana's emotional glow, more than once through her teenage years, before it was full strength, he knows, how intoxicating, how overwhelming it can be. He has also seen the carnage, helped Sarah mop it up, just like now. Oak calls Lockie back, he is dancing down the track and he is too far away now, too close to the lake. Lockie, who will repeat their warning as to the danger of the lake, will in the same breath, begin removing shoes and socks, jeans and underpants, shirt and hat because the lake is also so swimmable in. But not today, please not today, today is already too pregnant with drama.

Lockie waits, impatiently but waits. He begins singing.

"We are the pirates of the lake,"
"We are the pirates of the lake."

Lockie is forever inventing his songs, they are an abundance of inspiration and a precision of line, this one has exactly seven words which are both chorus and refrain. And he will sing it while they walk to the end of the track to the boat hire shed, the boat hire jetty and the boat hire boats. The boats are red and white, clinker built, they are pirate boats, so Lockie says, but not equally pirate boats. There is one which is especially a pirate boat and both Lockie and the boat hire man in dungarees and Greek sailors cap, both know which.

The boat hire man looks like his father, Allen had hired boats from his father, his own father had hired boats from this man's grandfather. Allen wasn't sure who his own Grandfather had hired boats from. He used to come here, to take the "radio active waters", (as the advertisement said) Grandpa Joske was a large man with a military moustache of another era. He wore tweed suits, pressed trousers, sturdy shoes and a golfers cap. He filled the rowing seat of the clinker boat, Allen and his brothers scrambled for the bow, just as Lockie does, giving directions to the aft facing rower. It is a small lake with the single feature of a small island, towards the northern shore. It is, of course a treasure island, "X" marks the spot. His own grandfather would never, himself, disembark on the island, as if it were too undignified for the English gentleman (he wasn't). He and Lockie do, despite the mud, the bulrushes, the quicksand and the possibility of monsters. They will find something to call a treasure.

"We are the pirates of the lake."
"We are the pirates of the lake."

He sings it in the solemn key of B flat.
"It is a kind of B flat day," Oakley says, and begins to giggle.

9. Mopping up

Sarah tries to talk sense to Diana.
"Please don't do anything rash. Please, please, please, please, don't do anything irreparable."
"You don't understand Mum, I don't know if I'm gay."

Sarah knew, after the Afghan, she needed to do something explosive. Sarah, wanted, desperately wanted, to think better of her youngest than that, but right at that moment, she didn't. She had been too enmeshed in the whole residency, visa, cock-up with Mohamed, the whole, coming out drama, with Anne, to just turn around and say, "Oh, by the way, I'm not gay anymore, it's too much, too bloody much." Sarah is angry, and she doesn't want that, anger's not helpful, not helpful today.

She doesn't want this to be about gay, she desperately wants this to be about Lock, it's about family, and the things which we do, to hold it together, and not let it fail.

"This will hurt Lockie, he's bonded with Oak, and Oakley with him, it's not a small thing."

"But I owe it to Lockie, to find who I am, what he needs is a mother, independent and strong."

Malissa's just staring at her sister right now, does she think we are all stupid? Does she think we can't see, straight through her flawed logic, to the heart of the thing? Diana is doing the same thing again, twisting the world to suit her own ends, using Lockie as a foil.

Sarah bites her lip, there are so many things she could say, the geomorphology of her brain is erupting with lava flows of "Things I should keep to myself" fissures of steam and turbulent cracks of surface. Not about the gay thing, that's just an excuse, just a red herring to disguise something else, what makes Sarah furious is that this involves kids, one kid, but one is enough. You are obligated to think clearly, when you rip at the fabric of other peoples lives.

Does she think I haven't been here and wrestled with this, divorcing Luke wasn't easy, with two tiny kids, and then all the dilemmas about being with; staying with All.

"You don't do this lightly, you think this stuff hrough."

"I've thought about nothing else for a month."

"I'm talking about family, not talking about you."

It's a distinction Diana doesn't get, and it grated her mother for a very long time. She ain't going to say, "stay for the kids," she wants to say something more subtle than that, she's not saying she stayed with All for the kids, but they were part of the equation, part of the glue, part of the reason to see this thing through, and part of the reason they have held it in place, and it worked for the better, they worked through their shit, enough, sometimes just enough, but just enough can sometimes be enough.

"Don't be too hasty, don't be too rash, this is the moment when you just have to breathe."

There is no good solution they can arrive at today, they agree that All and Sarah will take Lockie with them so she and Oakley can spend a week just the two of them to work some things out.

And it feels like Diana has got her own way again, extended the drama, extended the noise.

10. Lockie builds a Thing-a-me-jig

Lockie sings for an hour and sleeps for the rest. He's excited to be heading down to the beach, they can work in the workshop and keep building their thing. Lockie perched high on a stool near the bench, dangerously high, but that's Lockie's spot. It's the best place to help, holding the thing, or banging a bit, or using his screwdriver, his hammer or helping the most helpful way that he can, grandpa and Lockie building the "Thing-A-Me-Jig."

"It's time that we named it something better than that."

He switches the switch on, switches it off, plays with the dial, and bangs on the lid. Allen suggests he don't bang so hard, just so they finish it before it is broke. If they box up the circuits they might last for a while, though its the making what matters, their time at the bench. Boys doing boy things, just playing around, with bits of solder, and circuitry boards, old cigar boxes and spare bits of wood, and bits they have dug up from second-hand stores. And while All would have done the same for a girl, (had tried to with Di), it feels a fine symmetry that Lock is a boy, just like Sam, and him.

11. That Sam I Am.

Sam lives too far away. All the way to Apollo Bay, almost the complete length of the Great Ocean Road, carved into the cliff face in nineteen thirty-two, where the Otway hills tumble steeply into the Southern Ocean, the road winds around the cliff tops, a grey blue ocean heaves below, crashing waves. Occasionally the road descends to tiny hamlets hemmed by cliffs and walls of eucalyptus stands, beach and myrtle along the creeks, lush and wet from ocean storms. Allen Keys loves this road, it's drama, it's history and his history on it, he'd told Sarah the story of his riding his Moto Guzzi Le Mans along it in squalling rain, he totally mud squelched and his visor useless in the onslaught, he made it drenched to Apollo Bay just as the squall was easing. Or the time in stifling summer heat he'd driven the other way with Francis in the old "V-Dub-Per-U" a smoke haze circling just west of Lorne and then the fire, in the ridge tops high above, crackling, spitting, exploding, flames leaping south towards the road. We should have turned around of course, but we just kept driving. Allen Keys loves this road and so does his son.

Sam moved to Apollo Bay, four years ago, All and Sarah helped him buy the worst house in the worst street, just before the boom. He was lucky, a fibro beach shack, with a shed big enough to build his boards.

Lockie is singing a Lockie song in the back seat, he wants to know, "are we there yet," he wants to know when "will we get to music town?" It took them a while to realize he meant the festival, the Apollo Bay Music Festival, they went last year, and are surprised Lockie remembers. Sam lives in "music town."

It is a perfect late summer day; the Southern Ocean a pale pastel blue, high flimsy clouds on the west horizon and low dabs the highest ridges, misting the trees. The slightest sea breeze ruffles the swells, they drive through the bends slowly descending to the coast at Skenes Creek. They will meet at the surf club for an early lunch, what Sam actually said was, "Meet me at the office." The surf club is his office, his front of house, his sales room. Folks see him with his board and they want one, "the more I surf, the more I sell, it's the best business plan I know." Sarah is certain, if he surfed less he could make more, but, what the hell it works, and one of her frogs is happy enough in his pond for now.

Sam needs a haircut, Sam needs a shave, Sam needs some clothes that aren't seven years old. He looks like a wild man covered in salt, and sea and sun. He is a handsome man with a swimmer's body, he is better looking than All was at the same age; in All you could feel the caution, in Sam the passion pulsates.

They will eat fish and chips on the deck of the surf club, at least everybody but Sam will, Sam won't eat anything which comes from the sea, not even sea-weed. And after which Sam has promised Lockie a ride on the board. Lockie is almost too excited to eat, the surfboard is waiting and so is the sea.

There is a beach which is sheltered from the worst of the swells, it's a good beach to start on and in fact it's crowded with kids, none as young as Lockie, but the three of them will prevent him from falling as best as they can. The surfboard's enormous, for one little kid, if he kneels in the centre he shouldn't fall off. Sam held the board steady, then pushed it away, with Lockie on it in front of the wave, whoosh, went the surfboard and Lockie as well riding it the small distance into the shore. "Again", yelled Lockie, "Again" and "Again." And "Again" and "Again" and "Again" and "Again", until Lockie is shivering, with chattering teeth, "Enough," says Sarah, it's time to go back to Sam's workshop for biscuits and tea. Lockie is crying but Sam puts that right by promising his something he didn't expect. "We'll go back to the workshop and build you a board, but I'll need you to help me, it's a two-worker job."

Sam finds Lockie a box for some tools, a red box with a lid that doesn't quite fit, in it's a hammer, a spanner and pliers, two screwdrivers, an allen key, and an old hand drill without any bits. That's the best thing, you wind it and "wwwhhhrrr.......wwwhhhrrr.....wwwhhhrrrr!"

Sam's workshop is the opposite of everything Sam, it is pristine, it is neat, there is a place for everything and everything has a place. It is an assembly line, boards at every stage of construction are laid out on benches, when he cuts, he cuts the timber for more than one, when he assembles he assembles more than one, when he is clamping and gluing one he is working on another. He even has a white board with every board, every order and at what stage it is at. He writes "Lockie's Board" on his white board, it's officially begun.

Lockie draws a squiggle and picks up his drill.

12. Pizzas for Eight

Miranda is making pizzas and salad for everyone, the whole bloody family in Sarah's flat on Alexander Avenue. She and Sarah have invited everyone because it's a family thing. "And I'm being host because I am the boring one, the reliable one." And while Miranda would not like to live in Diana's constant drama, or play the beach bum, like Sam, sometimes she resents her casting. She is however and always will be, her father's daughter, "sans affairs". She was older when they were divorced and closer to her father, she is the only one who never lived down the beach, couldn't live down there, on the swamp land. She is the hard working one, the focused one, the steadfast one. She'd never had a stream of boyfriends, only one, who Diana stole, because she could, because it was so easy, what Miranda had struggled with Diana just took, took him, then spat him out. "Not really my type Miranda, he's much more yours."

"She may have saved me from myself, I'll never know."

Miranda turned her focus to the lens of an electron microscope, to the perplexing, fascination, uncertain world of research science, the familiar world of her parents. She has invited her father, "He is my father, he is Diana's father for Christ sake."

Miranda now accepts, that her mother is somehow better with All, but still feels some of the resentment, in herself and in her mother. Her mother has never completely reconciled her anger at Luke with her neat Jewish family. It was her father who told Miranda that she shouldn't expect it of Sarah. "There is a little bit of Diana inside your Mum, passionate, mercurial, explosive. She'll never completely forgive me, you know, and not because I fucked someone else but because I tore up her family." It would make Miranda's life easier if they could forgive and forget because she is the one in the middle, the one who is always slightly apart, uncomfortable, awkwardly, between and betwixted, the onlooker, not in the squabble. It can be lonely, and misunderstood, taken for granted, the wall-flower daughter, fading away, locked in her shyness and frightened.

Diana arrives first, she has promised to help with the pizzas, given she's decided to be vegan or veggo or something. She arrives bickering with Oakley. They are still bickering, surprisingly not about food, or Oakley's guns, or Diana's bitching about her Dad's new partner, or Diana's not having a job, or even a dedication, or a reason to be.

"But that's exactly what I'm talking about, if I could weld, I could make sculptors."

Oakley is trying to be calm. Oakley can weld, Oakley has an oxy-welder on the Anna Branch, Oakley could teach Diana to weld, for Christ sake she could do the welds for her.

"But can't you see Oakley, that's just you trying to be controlling. I have to own this."

She meant both figuratively and literally, and Oakley didn't need another cheap welder when Diana got bored, when her sculptors didn't win the right praise from the right people at the right time. And Oakley wasn't the right person, not today, not this week and not this month.

Diana hugs her sister, asks her if she knows when Mum will arrive with Lockie. "That's if All hasn't kidnapped Lockie."

Miranda asks her sister if she is still vegetarian.

"No, no, no, no, I'm vegan."

"And Anne?"

"Oaks a carnivore."

A beer swilling, gun tooting, whip cracking, rodeo going, country and Western listening, banjo playing, country girl. And just to prove it, she opens a beer, offering one to Miranda who politely declines and pours her and her sister a glass of Pinot Griggio. Oakley pulls up a bar stool and asks, "What to do?"

She looks good on a bar stool, beer in hand, and that's how Sam saw her for the very first time.

"Oh shit!" says Oakley, as Sam walks through the door.

"Oh shit!" says Sam, "That's the last thing I need."

They say it inside where no one can hear, but they scream it the instant they meet eye to eye.

The dyke is slightly shorter than him, spikey dark hair dyed blonde, a lithe body and a pixie face and a smile which bloomed for a moment, just a moment, forgetting herself.

Sam embraces his sisters, Diana then Miranda, always in that order. And Diana introduces him to "Oakley."

"Oakley?" He questioned.

"Annie, therefore Oakley because of the guns."

"What guns?"

"She's got a bloody arsenal."

"A pump action shotgun, an old twenty-two for the sheep and a three-o-three for the pigs, but I've gone off igs."

"For the sheep?"

"Sometimes you have to put them down, we don't like it but we have to. I've got a small flock."

"Merino or first cross?" Sam's head is full of questions and this, he knows is the stupidest.

"I'm the rogue daughter and I have a flock of rogue sheep, all of the orphans, the coloured, the blacks. Black sheep for the black sheep, it's a family joke."

She opens Sam a beer, she doesn't even ask.

Diana shrugs, she had expected Sam, Aussie surfer Sam to be discombobulated by Oakley, not sitting there, sharing beer, talking farming and making "their" pizza.

Sarah and Allen arrive with Lockie. Lockie wants Mum, then Oakley, then Sam to enquire about his surfboard.

"Me and grandpa are building a thing-a-me-jig."

"What does it do?"

"It makes noise."

Luke arrives with a bottle of Bannockburn Pinot Noir. He will share with Sarah and Allen. He will try to be good.

Melissa serves the pizzas on colour coded plates; red for the meat eaters, green for the seafood, orange for the vegans and yellow for the gluten free. Two salads, crispy bread and tapenade.

Sarah makes an effort to talk to Luke for Miranda's sake, Allen to talk to Miranda for Sarah. She can be difficult sometimes, always has been but not because they are not fond of each other rather because they are both at heart very private, somewhat shy and slightly awkward people.

As Sarah says, we do this because it is about family, but more family fugue than either family feud or family fold, everybody has a voice, no matter how skittish, no matter how shy.

13. The Heart Chakra

"We are not on the same page," Diana says to Talbert, "I mean I'm at yoga and she's at gun club. How is that supposed to work."

Talbert stroked his chin and looked the look which never failed, intense and sensitive in one. Ah! And so, it begins, with all of it's complications and all of it's fun and she is so gorgeous, a waste on a girl, he's doing her a favour, no, really, he is. He strokes his chin, he has an oriental style beard, wispy hairs of wisdom, whimsical hairs of love.

He speaks very softly and he speaks very close.

"You needed to explore, that side of yourself, it's what we do in yoga, open up ourselves to new possibilities, expanding our consciousness, embracing the world. My guiding sign is the heart chakra, I think yours is too."

"Bingo!" he has it, that's just who I am, "It's my heart that needs feeding, I just have to let it flow where it does." She can't help but feel that Oak is a dam, she's so solid and tree like, I used to like that in Oakley but now I can see, that kind of protection is imprisoning me. I think me and Oakley have lied to ourselves, about the gay thing and quite a bit more. In fact, Annie Oakley has never said that she was gay, exclusively gay, "It's about the person not the gender for me." She had a boyfriend in high school what does that say, and she hates her sly teasing, why does she say, there is yoga in shooting, the calm, single focus, the breath and the eye, the touch on the trigger, and the instant retort. The shot never lies; was I calm, was I focused, was I right in the moment, right in the now, the yoga of shooting, what a joke, what a scam.

So, unlike Talbert, who speaks from the heart.

"Namaste. Talbert."

"Namaste Di."

Oakley is exhausted. Tired of these conversations, tired of the justification, tired of half lies and the half truths running around and around in circles until you aren't sure which is which. Diana is very good at this, very practiced and Oakley isn't. Diana is being evasive, she is speaking yoga talk, she is exploring possibilities, she is opening chakras, she is finding her centre. She is doing so many wonderful things and Oakley is being prosaic for not seeing it. Oakley is seeing it, she is dumping Oakley for Talbert, full stop.

Oakley is pissed off nd Oakley is exhausted.

And Oakley has only one question, "Can I still see Lock?"

She can see Lockie, she can take Lockie to visit his uncle, a weekend away, now there is a joke, my surfie brother and my ex-girlfriend. It is a joke which allows her a weekend with Talbert, because not everybody loves other people's children. Talbert's ashram looks through the eucalyptus down to the blue green water of the lake, a glimpse through the trees but enough of a glimpse to see the row boats on the lake. Yoga class is over, people are leaving but not Diana, nothing which happens now will surprise either she or Talbert, not at least in it's outline maybe a little in it's detail. It doesn't surprise her that Talbert likes to remain behind the Yoga Master personae, he tells her little about himself and then only reluctantly. It doesn't surprise Talbert that Diana will want to get to know him. What does surprise him is that she is very good at it. He doesn't mind people knowing he comes from the Hartz River, it's one of his lines, one of his best lines, "my guiding sign is the Heart chakra because I was born on the Hartz." But he hadn't expected her to know where the Hartz is, "My Uncle used to fish there, he was in love with the Hartz." But that meant she knew that the only people who lived there were cattlemen, which made her guess who Talbert's family was. Talbert did not want to discuss his family, nor his family business. "I find it objectionable." As does Diana, and over a vegan feast of mushroom, buckwheat and organic penne pasta, they discussed how Annie had clung to "the girl from the bush, the whole Annie Oakley thing, akubra and guns."

Talbert wisely stroked the hairs on his chin, "She must have a fixed sign and roots deep in the earth."

"You know it is funny I called Annie "Oak" but that's exactly the person she is, she is strong and she's solid, an immovable force, but then she's inflexible, won't bend with the wind, she just says, "I'm happy with the girl that I am." (All of it Di, the hat and the guns, the love of the outback, the way that it is, I love who I am Di, I don't pick and choose, I am Annie bloody Oakley and I come with the lot.")

14. Annie Bloody Oakley comes with the Lot

In an old Holden Ute, she came with Lockie and she came with attitude. "I think what we need is to be straight from the start, there won't be any fucking and there won't be any us, this is about Lockie building his board."

Sam just smiles, shrugs and says, "Sure," in a slow south coast drawl. He offered Lockie lemonade and offered Oak beer, to have in the workshop and look at the board. He'd told her about the workshop and stuff but told is not seeing and seeing is "Wow!"

"And this is Lockie's surfboard, its beautiful Sam."

It's only just started but she means all the rest, they are all so damn elegant with the parquetry decks, all beautifully polished, they practically glow. He's even used marquetry to spell out his name.

Lockie wants to know if they can go surfing first, "Shall we, shall we, shall we" He says, well if this is about Lockie they suppose that they should. Sam asks Oakley to stand and turn around as he critically eyes her, short, lean and lithe, a little bit boyish, but less than he thought.

"It's traditional mate to check out the teeth."

He ignores her, he's thinking, "I guess you'd fit." His old wet suit he'd worn when he was a youth. "It will be tight in some spots and too loose in some but sure as hell better than freezing to death."

But Oak's not that stupid, he was checking her out, "and what about Lockie, should he turn around too."

"Lockie's a kid and kids don't get cold, but I've got him a "rashie" and a pirate life jacket, with a bold pirate flag."

They change in the surf club and meet on the beach. Lockie's excited, he's running away. Oakley yells, "stay", but Sam intervenes, lifting him up, and swinging him round, then dumping him down beside the board on the beach.

"First you have to learn to sit on the board."

"I can sit."

"No Lockie, this is important, you must sit the right way, if you don't sit correctly you'll never stand up."

And while he is about it, he taught Oakley too. They play on the shel-tered beach in small shore-break waves, Lockie being held up by Oakley and Sam, he constantly falls off, and constantly bobs his head above water to yell, "Again and again!" and not even once does he sit how he's shown. Until Sam pulls him off and wrapped in a towel a shivering Lockie plays sand-castles instead while Oakley tries surfing, "It's a very stable board, I should know cause I built it, with my very own hands."

And that's the thought which struck her as the waves washed her in, he bloody well built this, "how good is that!"

Later in the workshop they talk to each other, while Lockie, exhausted sleeps on a couch. Stories of the Anna Branch, and how they grew up, to be the two people who meet here and now.

15. I am a Botticelli Angel and I Play This to Win

It's not a conversation that working well for Di, Talbert's being evasive, defensive, except about the rules. His rules are clear, well thought out and precise. "I don't do domestic, it is stifling Di. I need to keep it free, I need to keep it fluid, I need to keep it pure."

He emphasized, "Pure."

"Spiritually Di, we have to meet there, we aren't mundane people, we have travelled too far on the path of evolution. We have reached higher planes."

Diana smiled her most beloved of smiles, and let him talk on all his spiritual guff. Whatever he says, whatever he thinks. She likes him. She wants him. She gets what she wants. He might know yoga, but so far he ain't playing this game as hard as he should. Diana says to Diana, under her breath.

"I am a Botticelli Angel and I play this to win."

16. The God of Dysfunctional Love

Sarah held the two wires together for Allen who with solder in one hand and soldering iron in the other, needs two more hands to get this just right. The two wires which will give him the needed note "G". She has come to the workshop because she is worried about Di, worried about Sam and that peculiar girl Oak.

"I am not sure what to think of it all, this one really out of the box. Can you see anyway this can end well?"

Allen can see many, many endings, most of them disastrous he'll have to admit, except, "I really do like her and I know that Sam does."

"But what is going to happen in a year or in ten when she turns to Sam in tears and says, I just can't pretend that I can be with you Sam, as much as I love you, this whole boy, girl thing. It's really not me, you have to see that."

"I think we are getting ahead of ourselves, as far as we know, they are no more than friends."

Sarah cannot believe this man is so dumb, she smiles at Allen and says to herself, "Let us pray to the God of Dysfunctional romance that we have at last some peace, a few months at least." And she sits there waiting for another phone call, traditionally from Diana, but maybe from Sam.

17. Ring, Ring.

Sarah reluctantly answers the phone. It is Miranda and she will need all her strength.

STORIES FROM THE
SEA AND SHORE

Memoirs of a Binocular'd Girl

On the harbour white linocut yachts skid into jibes around the buoys and passed the lighthouse, sails in the fickle breeze, scenting changes. Poppy watches in the pale day through her father's binoculars, the boy in the red sailed mirror, wee in the distance, furthest of them all. She, thinking of yesterday when they'd walked around the lighthouse cape to the glass pools, they'd hunted crabs under barnacled rocks and saw sea-anemones, red and purple with delicate tentacles. The boy said they would grab your fingers if you brought them near, she didn't, or only teasingly, smiling her quick eyes. They caught the crabs with red freckles, their hands jumping from claws, crabs scurrying to safer rocks and they laughed and were happy yesterday. But mostly with this boy it is like now, he distant and wee, except in another harder way.

He comes now, running the wind, sails peacocked on a by-himself sea, the way he loves to sail, and the way in which he hasn't the sureness to live. At least that's what Poppy thinks, watching him in the binoculars, seeing the waves flesh threshing, but not hearing their gurgling effervescent sounds.

"Tomorrow," says the boy, lying in the sand, his hair gringly with salt, "I'm going to sail even further."

"Then I'll need a telescope."

"No," he says, "Further than a telescope."

"Oh," says Poppy, looking at him lying in the sand, "Why don't you lie on my towel, you'll get sand everywhere?"

"If you like," he says so casually that she slaps him lightly on the shoulder to get some reaction, but doesn't.

Tomorrow; the boy uncoils a small red sail, loads into his yacht, a water bottle, a few oranges and a jumper then pushes himself into a quill sea to find some wind. Poppy sits on top of a dune and watches him through the binoculars, tack the Mirror into one then another quarter of bay seeking the breeze. "So this is how men go to sea," she says to herself with a lithe laugh. But near the lighthouse he finds the winds beginning, his red sail ballooned, sailing further than her binoculars into the uncertain melt of sea and sky.

Poppy rolls onto her back, takes a cap out of her red beach bag and puts it on under a ripening sun, she begins to read a book he'd given her called, "The Merry-Go-Round in the Sea", that's what the yachts do, merry-go around the buoys, she'd said, and he'd said, "Yes," without agreeing. They always did this, lay on the beach, a book each so they could read between swims. Poppy wouldn't read and he wouldn't talk, except to tell her what he liked in a book and what he didn't. "The Merry-Go-Round in the Sea", should have more yachts in it somewhere", he said when he gave it too her. She supposed his reading was why he knew so many unimportant things, yet things no one else ever told her, like the day at the rock pools, he'd told her of the sea shells with firing spears and thin fishing lines, although instead of listening she'd licked the salt off the back of his shoulders and laughed, for she doesn't always believe the things he tells her. All day and all evening he remains out to sea, while Poppy paddles in the shallow water, lies under the sun and coaxes her father when he comes to the beach, into the brine with tales of how sparkly it is.

"Where is Clive?" asks her father.

"He's sailed out to sea."

"Will he want dinner? I'm cooking schnapper."

"No, he's too far out to sea."

Clive didn't get in for schnapper, his favourite food and by dusk her father was worried.

"He should be in by now", says her father, watching a vacant horizon from the house balcony through his binoculars.

"He will be alright," says Poppy, "He is good with boats."

"Yes", says her father, "He is."

He is good with boats, Poppy thinks in the morning.

Watching from the top of the dune the other yachts merry-go-round the buoys, and thinking of the things she has done with him. The day of the fine mist rain when he took her fishing on the cause-way, but they caught nothing and she even lost her hand-line, so they walked back to where the fishing boats unloaded their netted hauls and watched the fishermen while they ate fish and chips. How much they laughed at themselves that day: how wonderful it is to laugh like that. And the evening he took her to watch the shearwaters returning at dusk from the mauve sea, gathering in giant wheels in the air, "They are smelling for their nests", he'd told her and she laughed until she tried to think of any other way they could find them on the grey spinifex cape. They lay flat and close in the spinifex grass while the birds wheeled, flapping, frantic above them. It was, she always said, "what brought them together, lying still in the spinifex", then she smiled cynically at that. She thinks, that would be a good thing to do today, walk around the lighthouse cape, listening to him tell her about the things the waves have washed and later to watch the great flocks come in from the dark sea, but he also is out to sea and Poppy begins to feel the loneliness of that.

Poppy gets up and wanders down to the water, the sea, blue, but not her opal blue dispirits her as if she expected to find something she'd want to ask the meaning of, and that only adds edge to her loneliness. So instead of going swimming she walks up to the house where her father is standing on the balcony scanning the horizon through his binoculars.

"I haven't spotted his sail."

"No", says Poppy.

"I've told the Coast Guard", her father says in a kind, serious way.

"He is not lost", says Poppy, sitting on the deck chair, wrapped in a green towel. "It's cooler up here", she adds irrelevantly to her father still looking at the horizon.

Somewhere, somebody will be looking for him. Poppy thinks, looking at her toes which have a thin film of skin joining them to the first joint. "I'm kind of like a duck", she thinks and they won't find him.

In the afternoon, when the breeze comes back from the sea, she grows very sad. In a way, she thinks, that is stupid, for if he were here he'd sit on the other deck chair watching the yachts and he wouldn't say anything to her, even if she took his hand or smiled her funniest smile. He'd only grin back annoying her with his other distance. Yet it made her very sad that this sea breeze didn't bring him back this wax paper afternoon. And that night when her father took her to watch the Shearwaters as she'd asked him to she didn't believe him anymore about them smelling for their nests.

Poppy wished to sleep the next morning away but woke at dawn and went down to the bay. He wasn't there. She couldn't think of anything to fill today except waiting. Remembering or trying to, the way the wind blew the day of the glass pools or the day of the fine rain or even the evening of the Shearwaters, but she couldn't remember and he'd always spoken of the wind in that special way of sailors. She tries to remember again but it is even vaguer, so she has a shower and lies on her bed reading a book she doesn't like, waiting for the afternoon.

Finally it comes; the afternoon, the wind off the sea, the red speck of sail, and the boy, burnt red from the sea, his hair glued with salt.

"I'm hungry", he says like Ulysses.

"Dad's cooking Bream."

"Not schnapper?"

"You missed the schnapper."

And while he rolls up his red sail he says to her, "There wasn't anything except the sounds of the waves I love to hear and after a while they didn't sound at all."

Poppy smiles faintly at him and thinks to herself that from today she'll have to begin learning to live without this boy.

The Bay of Islands

"Always wanted to see a whale on the islands."

Mallee thinking, there has to be whales.

"You's born there Mallee, know there aren't any."

There were dead whales, two had washed up on the islands in a week. Mallee was going back to the islands, to Noel's, who would know about the whales. Jess drove the old Peugeot fast. Mallee lay across the seat, feet to arse, head elbow'd watching spinnaker branches pass, pass, like pianola holes. The islands would have whales.

Jess turned the Peugeot into a bend, looked, a vagrant grin, across the dash to Mallee.

"You're weird Mallee ……" Jess thought, "cause you drank too much sea water …… swam too much, out to the islands, that was looney."

Forest rain, giraffe close and summer. Jess reckoned "looney" the wrong word. He guarded that swim, in a storm swelled ocean out to the furthest of the three islands. He'd always wanted one of them to swim too. And knew, only Mallee could swim it. Mallee tilts a bottle of beer to his mouth, brown colour, suns codes of light. Remembering Jess's rites of dare and double dare, and the naked, testicle swim to the furthest island. Something like fear, slower than fear, lonelier than fear. The island felt, cape like without land, forlorn in it's secretive kemp wet tides.

Jess says, "Bet no ones swum it since Mallee."

"Maybe a whale."

"Na ….. no ones swum it."

***

Slow falling turns, ragged brushed mist, shrill bell-bird cry, grey sad ash. Cigarette ash falls to Mallee's grey linen shirt, he brushes it off or in with a flick of his bottled hand, pastures, rye grass, spiked yellow.

The Peugeot sounds, gallop, gallop over a plank bridge. A water splash, egret flies, swirls and lands further a narrow tossed creek. Mallee's head out of the open car window, watching the egret, it's strange gulp of neck, hesitant foot forward landing. A weird crab eating bird, weird as whales, as Jess thought Mallee. Mallee thinking a whale must swim to the islands to die there.

A heath coast, layers of mist just above the ocean discolours it, dents of blue, lighter blue, storm above them moving.

"Storm coming."

Mallee gulps beer.

"Mallee don't drink sea water no more, drinks beer."

Light rain.

Jess grins.

A fallen dark kernel of storm crawls over the heath cliffs. Heavy rain moths the Peugeot's fenders, through Mallee's open window, flicking Mallee's flaxen clumps of hair.

***

Grey-black clouds low and tattered over Noel's Bay of Islands house, a different wind whine of high pines. A wooden box of apples, kitchen pots, a jean jumped girl, "Robin" says Noel, arm over Mallee's shoulder.

Hair fine lines of face, elfin, she glanced at Mallee, wary. Mallee split fire wood. Noel ways says, "a fire for his spirit," laughing like he knew his spirit a humorous bloke.

Noel's face deep in the chip wood stove, blowing, shudders fire through damp wood, fire moving. Noel yarned about the orchard wood.

"Doesn't pay much, won't be much work before the end of summer."

This is summer on the South coast.

Mallee who'd quit his city job, told them.

Robin asks dryly, "What are you going to do?"

"Dunno," Mallee's face shrugs, "wanted to come back to the islands."

"Mallee wants to see a whale."

Noel, who'd know about the whales, sits in an old cushioned chair across from Robin and the chip wood stove. Mallee watches Noel, to tell him about the whales. Noel shoves wood into the fire. Looks at Mallee, puzzling.

"Ain't seen a whale."

"Must have seen the dead ones."

"Yeah, seen them."

Mallee , hope pries Noel. Noel thumb angles fingers along his mouths break, eyes his head towards Mallee.

"Dead ones, maybe they float in dead from Antarctica."

Jess laughs.

Mallee can feel the islands whale filled seas.

"Sharks would get them before they floated in dead from Antarctica."

Mallee, Noel, reckon agreement about the sharks. Robin, leg up on Noel's chair, one leg pinned under the other, bridged, a buckled paper face on her knee. Mallee despondent knowing, whales must be there if they die there.

Jess jokes, "oughta take Mallee's boat to Antarctica, sank more places than anyone fished."

Mallee would row it out, swim it in ….. and tales of Island's over-times conversed into the afternoon.

Jess left. Mallee opens the house paddock gate, wind calm, sun. Mallee walks down the fields mud slipping slopes. Noel to redraw stories of Mallee, less weird than before. A Mallee who arrived.

"He's not that weird."

"Weird enough."

"Chopped the wood."

Robin says cautiously, "Guess so." and "Where has he gone?"

"Gone off."

Mallee went off, over road fence down to the islands, the smaller islands and the furthest massive swam to island. A slow breathing sea, thrust massive waves to the bay cliff edge. Mallee jeans wet to the knees, the water still summer warm.

Small storm chop ridges across a deeper ocean swell, white break-ers like whales.

Whale thoughts.

They die here.

Mallee swimming the empty triangle of the Bay of Islands, a feeling so close to fear.

Waves, spray stung Islands, holed hulls of rock. Every wave invents a word, wave words, wailing words, song.

"A whale song."

"There aren't any whales …… a mellow-choly song."

Mallee's mellow-choly song. The island called, something like a whale song in the islands forlorn, whaleless bay.

In A House of Geckos

Ree says to Gecko; the reason she loved his father was because she knew he was a dolphin. Geckos looks at his mother with still black globe eyes, she rubs antiseptic into his ankle where a bull-ant had bittern him and he'd scratched until it bled, white antiseptic which doesn't hurt, red antiseptic looks like it hurts. The television is on Huckleberry Hound.

Ree has spoken to Gecko in this way since they'd left the house near the sea - the brown wood house with cane blind light, straw brown spinifex grass and people brown with sun. The house where geckos crawled up the walls, with the blink, blink, blink of the lighthouse at night in the straights, and in the day the many blues of sea and sky. And now they live in a house which faces the Porongorup hills, a green house.

"Mum." Gecko asks; he is called that because he used to catch geckos with a flick of hand and show Ree their brown florescent bodies glistening like Cannabis sativa oil.

"Why don't we swim at Emu beach?"

Ree looks sad and doesn't answer. All last summer with Cress and Annette they would swim at Emu Beach, lie on the grass under Norfolk pines above the stone wall, and around the cool concrete outside showers. Gossiping, wrapping brown bodies into yellow towels, their hair clinging helmets to their heads. (Gecko would roll his towel above his head like a Bedouin.) Watching, below the wall, spinifex, sand and sea, the young men they talked about in their pleasurable way.

All last summer was spent in that flippant, easy swim and at the end of summer Gecko took to the water like a dolphin. Ree was desolate - his father is a dolphin - and he'll leave her for the sea. Neither said anything, they watched the shadows of the Norfolk pines come down onto the beach and Ree decided she'd leave the house by the sea, so Gecko would forget he is a dolphin.

Some stupid shows come on television, Gecko doesn't concentrate on. Ree is making dinner. When they are eating Cress comes, which isn't as usual as in the old house. She says, "Hallo," to Gecko who has a mouthful of potato. She sits near him, she doesn't smell the same as Ree, she has colours around her eyes and she has a dress on and Ree only has jeans and a T-shirt.

"We don't see you around?" Cress says to Ree.

"No."

"You ought to come out ….. to the west."

When Ree last went out it was to the Swan Reach, and they wore jeans and T-shirts. Ree hadn't a dress of fine cotton, hand printed in Bali like Cress. She didn't know they wore things like that.

"I might."

"On Friday."

Cress looks at Gecko who has finished eating his potato and is shoveling left-overs around his plate with a spoon.

"What's Gecko been doing?"

"I got bitten."

Ree is watching Cress, she says, "a bull-ant bit him." But she is thinking of the old house, the red, green striped deck-chairs where Cress and her and sometimes Annette sat facing an evening wind shift off the straight, eating cantaloupe and mandarins, talking about who was at Emu Beach and who was not and what who wore, where they got the cloth from for her sarong and why these mandarins are so sweet. However much it didn't feel like it - that was this Cress - and that was this Ree.

After Cress left Ree thought she shouldn't have agreed to go to the West.

She says, "I'd like a dress like that."

Probably to Gecko watching television in the room zinc from gun smoke light, far outside the crash, sink, crash of a mauve black sea.

Gecko wakes in the first light and wakes Ree for his breakfast of left to get milk-logged "wheat-bix" left to get cold toast. Left because the day is so interesting with parrots in the yard.

Ree takes Gecko out to see them; they flock across the yard near the flame red Christmas trees, they are crimson and topaz and screech, parrot squawks, which sound as if they are saying, "the dolphins are swimming in, the dolphins are swimming in!" Ree is astounded and disturbed, she holds Gecko close. Gecko stares at the parrots.

"They know my farther?"

A parrot tilts its head and neck feathers towards Gecko in that strange parrot way as though it were made of plastic tubing and can move its head around and around without it plonking off.

"Yes," it squawks, "The dolphins are swimming in."

Then the parrots fly off to a wheat harvest. Gecko stares after them. His smooth, round, dark eyes focus into the holes the parrots sky'd.

Ree says, "the parrots are mimics."

"What is a mimic."

"They only repeat what others say."

The dolphins are swimming in, all the signs are there and Ree knows them all; the Christmas trees flowering, the ocean swells becoming sharper and faster, her favourite blue in sky and sea, or at least it used to be. She didn't want Gecko to know, these parrots, she thinks, are a dolphins doing.

Ree says, "you play inside today so you won't get bitten."

And because clouds in the west rehearse storms for the coast.

"Will the parrots come back?"

"No."

Inside Gecko discovers sheets drying over a cloths hoist, filter the blue and white light of a benevolent drollness sea. He swims within it, knowing the dolphins are swimming in. And when the storm comes, a storm Ree would have watched in the old house, the way it rakes across the straight, the way it makes her feel at sea, Gecko's skin turns dolphin. Ree watches frantic, his mouth grow peaked, his eyes move backwards to disappearing ears, hands web, legs join and feet swivel outwards, by evening he is half dolphin. At first Ree weeps, then she grows angry, at the dolphin who is making this happen; who is claiming her son. She grows angrier and angrier until she knows she must do something - she must confront the dolphin.

Ree puts on a yellow oil skin coat for the storm, runs down Adelaide hill, across Emu Point Road where in summer their sandals sizzle on hot bitumen, to the lawn and the Norfolk pines of the foreshore. There is a large storm break, the dolphin keels instinctively through and over its crest and into the next break.

Ree screams at the dolphin, "Why have you done it?"

The dolphin submerges and reappears where Ree is standing crutch deep when the waves break. There is something confused in his face and wishing in his voice.

"Ree?"

"Why have you done it to Gecko?"

"Gecko."

"Your son …. why have you made him a dolphin?"

The dolphin is puzzled. He looks at her, Ree's hair is plaited by the storm, how the oil skin coat looks almost dolphin. (Why did she name him after a reptile?)

"I haven't made him a dolphin."

"You have to stop it ….. you have to make him a son again."

The dolphin looks at her sadness, and although there is nothing he can do to make Gecko human again, he says, "Bring him here, maybe there is something."

"You will take him."

Ree is in panic. The dolphin sees an apology on Ree's face - in lips and eyes that wishes some things not said. She goes back to the house where Gecko is a dolphin, carries him heavily back down Adelaide hill to Emu Beach and down to the water. But when Gecko touches the water they can see there is nothing to be done. Gecko takes to the water, he swims the same dive, break, dive as his father.

His father thinks in his strange dolphin way. "We cannot change him from a dolphin ….. but maybe we can change you to a dolphin."

He stops; watches Ree. Ree looks at her human times - in the old house with the geckos climbing up the walls, if there were more of those summer times of seemingly endless swim, but no. Gecko is a dolphin. Ree dives into the waves, feels her feet enormous, unaccustomed thrust which makes her almost backflip, until she gets used to it. Until she, Gecko and the dolphin, surface, dive and surface towards the blink, blink, blink of the lighthouse in the straight and Ree all the time wondering if dolphins ever tasted anything as sweet as a mandarin?

The Master of the Melancholy Carp

"Fine weather for sailing." Malone says.

The Captain looks over the half-moon tides of the D'entrecasteaux Channel to every island framed glint of water from where he stands in black currant bushes to the slender blue horizon of the Tasman sea. High clouds - Cirrocumulus; he watches them coming nor-west.

"Fine weather for sailing," the Captain agreed.

He ships his hand across the black currant branches, dropping leaves and currants into a large steel pan dumped between his knees, cragged out of torn dungarees. He tosses the pan, black currants and leaves fly into a nor-west breeze - a leaf spray and the currants, but not the leaves fall back into the pan, being heavier like gold in a gold pan. The Captain is the Captain because he has always owned ships, (boats at least) from his far childhood; to the boat, he assured Malone, that lazed in moorings under those high clouds in the D'entrecasteaux Channel.

"A boat," the Captain once said, "Is like your strength or your saviour" (And he laughed in this Seventh Day Adventist black currant plot) "Come anything, floods, earthquakes or a job as poor as this you can always get away in a boat."

Malone had thought - cyclones- but forgot those as he watched a small white fishing boat, with slow chug-chugging motor (Like a heartbeat) and unmenacing wake, ride the channel out to sea. Out to sea, that is what he and the Captain will do away from the black currant picking - bush to pan to air to pan to bin, a five gallon bin which holds twenty five kilograms of black currants, worth to Malone and the Captain twenty dollars a hundred kilograms. Yesterday Malone and the Captain picked thirty kilograms, because, as they are told, they are riffraff and sinners who wouldn't work to save themselves (bless the lord) and because the black currant plot is too high in the hills, it's fruit frost bruised and scarce in rock boned clay. They are filling the base of their bins with rocks, hill clay, water to add weight without work but the boss knew every weight adding trick a sinner might use.

The Captain is worse than a sinner, he has deserted his decent friend Joe - who spends his time pushing the stalks back into the raspberries and laughing at his joke (he cannot do this to the black currants and has been sad these black currant days) and taken up with the riffraff and main-lander Malone, all because of Malone's puzzling weather reports. Puzzling because Malone doesn't have a radio or any other vehicle of prediction. The Captain said, he could use a man like that on the ship and took up with Malone, which is what Malone wanted.

Malone has a lighthouse - not a real, red and white striped lighthouse with round yellow weather beacons but something better. Maybe the other pickers eyes are not as young for no one else has noticed it - across the channel on a small promontory a man flys paper carp from tall flag-poles; on this fine day, a red, white and blue flapping carp, blue and gold on windier days, orange and red on even windier days and on stormy black days, no carp at all. This is Malones weather forecast, his passage on the boat and his way out of here.

Malone sifts leaves from the currants with purple currant fingers - he has given up trying to throw the pan. He stops and rolls a cigarette and the Captain rolls one too.

The Captain says, "On me ship, I've got proper tobacco."

Maybe Malone thinks his own tobacco.

The Captain had everything on his ship from his beer to his only usable frying pan. It was just down there in the channel, down in Cygnet bay, you can't spit into it, it isn't as close as it looks, it looks like you could spit into it. Sometimes Malone wishes the Captain would bring his things up from the ship, then he thought of the inconvenience of it, how he would probably have to help and he didn't wish it anymore.

Malone says, "We sailing soon?"

"Yep, soon."

Behind them is another voice, high and nasal. "You two gunna work today, gunna act like decent people or employment service riffraff.?"

Malone had come up from the Hobart employment service and he was a mainlander, the Captain used to be decent. The Captain sits legs towed into the clay, back against the currant bushes he says, "Bastard," then, "If he was on me ship."

And thinks of keel-hauling, hanging from the top gallant, while Malone throws black currants and leaves into the air then spends twice as much time as he should trying to pick the currants out of the clay where once again they land instead of in the pan. It is while Malone is picking the currants out of the clay that he finds the first spud.

"Spuds!" he says.

"Eh?"

"Spuds," says Malone, "The mud's rocky with spuds."

The Captain kicks his boots into the clay, a couple of spuds unearthed.

"Christ, we're carrying a cargo of spuds."

The Captain digs into the black currant clay pulling spuds from the hold.

"Malone bins."

The black currant picking bins to hold the spuds. Malone runs down to the old Ferguson tractor and it's trailer of bins. He grabs three, clangs them up to the Captain who has burrowed yards of spuds. Malone piles them into the bins.

"Boss will be properly angry now."

The Captain is frozen in digging, he says, "We're sailing."

He says it like enlightenment.

Before sailing - Malone sits in the rust iron picker's hut, the furthest away from everyone's riffraff hut. The Captain cooks spuds with tomatoes fetched from the Adventist garden. He drinks a bottle of Malone's Cascade beer. They eat this good lunch, Malone thinking of the sea's murky tides, where they are going with spuds and beer, maps and charts (whatever the difference).

There is yelling from the boss's house, then a bullet twines across their roof. The Captain jacks out of the shack. It is the boss's boy, a fourteen year old dollard's face splattered with black currant freckles and vacant eyes, he is on the hut track, yelling for them to come out like he is in a cheap Western movie.

The Captain races at the boy, dodging hut to hut. The boy stands his ground then runs too late from the quicksilver Captain who gets the boy down, cursing with his toothless mouth the boy's idiot face. The Captain and Malone drag the kid between them, the boy's feet swimming down the deck, down the hut track to a dam below Malone's hut. An iron sheet irrigation pump house, a tank on uneven trestle of wood and a planked irrigation pipe jutting into the dam something like a pier leading to an old half sunken dingy. The Captain drags the boy out over this hoists him two handed by ripping shirt and throws him into the water, before plonking himself into the vessel.

The kid sprawls, belly flops into the dam's black glint water. He surfaces, spitting water, swearing, he'll bloody kill them next time, "sinners!"

The Captain looks like sailing. He stands in the boat over the dam's water tide of sea. Malone crawls along the plank, pipe, pier, unsure of sailing. the Captain watches the tide ebb, rising in the dam's distant shore, building swells, all the way to the islands. Malone watches the melancholy carp master, small and dressed in black, come from his house, untie the carp and pull them in, folding them like the top hat he should be wearing - now as the next bullet squalls south-west and Malone's weather changes before the Captains determination and the dam's obstinacy.

STORIES FROM
THE ESTUARY

The Want Buyer and Crocodile Eye

Allie sits on the verandah room stretcher bed, looks at Jess lazily hot and hungover, looks to where below in the estuary crabs like crocodile eyes float on thin lips of low tide water. She wonders why the crabs migrate across the tidal mud down to the channel, why they don't live in the channel. And she also wonders why Jess has let him come back, this time like the last time?

Allie's hand turns the edge of a swearing Matisse red dress under her crutch. She asks Jess, why the crabs follow the tide down to the channel.

Jess says, "They never expect the water to go out."

She sits solemn. Pursed stretched face, eyes lowered with a scratch of tease (Allie could never be perfectly solemn.) The sun broke into the verandah room; green submarine light. She traces the suns shadows with tight muscle legs, thinking Jess would never expect the water to go out. All she knows of Jess, a hollow sense of what she doesn't know, says that. And says; Jess is futile to her leaving, although Allie doesn't think that.

Allie grins nervously and says, "I think the crabs are going to rescue the falling water."

They weep brittle tears.

Jess grins tensely, but grins. It severs the tautness.

"We gunna unpack your stuff?"

Allie has brought a carpet bag, a much used, tan, leather strapped case. She opens them, takes a few cloths out and piles them on the stretcher bed. Then she stops, not feeling like unpacking. She kicks her legs to annoy Jess. He ignores her, immersed in thoughts of keeping her, going to places she'd like to go to; the pub, estuary and ocean beach. And thoughts below those, that he shouldn't have let her come back. Allie kicks her other leg higher, rolling backwards tumbling across the stretcher bed, blankets and clothes onto the floor.

She laughs a jeckellish laugh.

Allie pulls Jess off his rigid chair and thoughts, she lifts her tight muscular body and sits cleft over him.

"We will do good things this time."

They lie in the tree scattered light of the verandah room. Sun crinkles across the estuary, tonight they will go to the Barwon Heads Pub, (always referred to as the B.H.P.) a good thing, Allie likes. His eyes map Allie's knees, where thigh and calf muscle twist, her deep blue eyes filament burns. Jess knows his besottedness can do nothing else but let her back, even for these few days she will stay to do as before, good things.

***

Through the pub windows near their table; a night's dark brooding, orange estuary bridge before equally dark stretch of ocean. Their table is away from a dull lit bar where fishermen shoal around. Jess tells Allie about the few things that have happened. Ocean storms, seen pelicans, even whales and occasional orchard work. He tells her, he is glad she is back but doesn't ask for how long. And he tells her about the estuary fishermen she likes to hear about.

"That bloke, fishes all day just along the bridge. He never catches anything."

Allie looks at him sadly. She likes to catch fish, most of these blokes don't. Jess sensed they fished to look into brown estuary waters because they had walked off bust farms or fishing boats they could no longer afford nets for; to live off susso and an impossibility to do anything else.

He tells Allie this.

She says, she'd be sick of farming after so many years. Allie speaks in her exuberant way, rattling on from a glass of Bourbon about the estuary crocodile eye crabs. Watches Jess for differences to the passive laziness of his face. There are none, he sits drinking beer, slowly and fallow, he could be a farmer and he'd never walk off. (She forgets in his way he is.)

Jess talks now, also about the crabs. It seems Allie's new curiosity and his one small fisherman's hope of keeping her.

"They weep the water at dawn, the hunting time."

He pauses, watching Allie's interest in her own idea. Trying to think of what should follow. She sits with her cotton dress tent between her legs, tight legged on a half-moon knee and intent.

"When the river came to comfort a first crocodile's tears, it ate the river. In revenge, the river washed away the crocodile body, overtime the river washes the body away the eyes remain weeping for their bodies."

Allie says, "Bull-shit!"

Jess doesn't know where that came from, there is a crocodile lake further up the river, and he'd wondered.

Allie says, "We will drop my crocodile into the river."

Allie's cast iron crocodile, Jess had brought it for her. It is really a nut-cracker with crocodile cracking jaws. Crocodile eyes floating crab like on cast-iron head. To test Jess's tale. Allie is already imagining it's body being washed away by the river, perkily with crazy Allie's trace element grin.

"When is the hunting time?"

"Dawn," says Jess, feeling a little like a fool.

***

A soggy mescaline shot dawn.

The hunting time flushed into the estuary. Allie cold in cotton dress holds the crocodile and walks in front of Jess over the heath banks of the storm livid estuary, to a rock wall sliced grey from grey-blue. Jess stands on the wall, his soul ebbing with channel tide. Allie walks across the tidal mud down to the channel. She bends her knees to the waves, holds her dress above the spat spray. Her hand and crocodile dangling above the water. A moment's wait, then the crocodile falls through the loose waves, rolls and dives down to the mud estuary bottom. It settles on the bottom, not reptile like, floating eyes ceiling the water but cast-iron and static on a brown mud bottom.

Allie waits for the river to wash away the crocodile body. To dissolve it leaving two crab eyes, weeping brittle waves.

It doesn't happen.

And they leave, Jess carrying a dripping, estuary wet but still same crocodile.

***

In the estuary room, Jess tells Allie, why the crocodile didn't disappear. Jess is being weird.

"The estuary feuds with the wind, when you are fighting you don't notice crocodiles."

Allie drew her fingers and thumb over her hair. Her hair flips at the edge of her forehead, it is a kind of committal.

She says, "Maybe tomorrow it will be calm."

Black morning queues of westerly squalls, for three days then a rouge daubed dawn, over a flat estuary. On mist wet heath, Allie follows Jess down to the estuary's stretched cellotape channel. A washed pastel faith and sad, Jess watches Allie roll jeans over her knees, crocodile stabbed inside her arm.

Allie's legs buckle the channel's flatness. She pushes the crocodile into the water. It sinks, minute explosion puffs of river mud. It lands and settles, a same cast-iron crocodile.

***

Allie leaves the crocodile on the veranda room window - where it can see the crabs it should be, she says and laughs her jeckelish laugh. She isn't worried that the crocodile didn't disappear or at least not as much as Jess. Jess is the serious silent that Allie doesn't like. It is not the right way to end the game, and it was a good game. She knows it is his way of not telling her that he is thinking of the crocodile and her, for him, it wasn't a game but a hook.

They walk down to the estuary, it is evening, the estuary flat and cold as the sun leaves and mist rises from the mangrove banks. A ground mist hazes the estuary, palms on the opposite bank look even tropical in the days last brightness.

Allie says, "It looks crocodile."

And then she is sorry that she said it.

At the pub ocean window table, Francis is there, Francis who Jess doesn't want to see (It's complicated) but who wants to meet Allie. A hair strangled Francis; frail white skin, touchless "Tilley Lamp" mantle colour wearing a brown jumper with sleeves too long for her arms and thin etching of her jeaned legs. Francis the consoler when Allie last left, but also Francis who believes in legends as transient, as touchless as herself. She reads the constellations she cannot recognize in a night's sky as clear as this, September's Scorpio falling. Francis's eyes shark Allie.

Francis moves around the table to where Allie sits crouched. Jess is annoyed at her being here and says little. Allie talks to Francis about the cast iron crocodile, estuary and crabs. Francis smiles wryly, like she knows Jess better than Allie and says slowly as word part.

"It's Jess, the wind cannot feud with the estuary, they're both Piscean."

It cannot be true but it stings Allie. Jess notices this. He wants them to leave but he doesn't ask. Allie sits drinking, knees up to her chin biting her Bourbon glass. Allie always quickly giddy with Bourbon thinks Francis and Jess know similarly strange things. It appeals to her whimsy, their strangeness, and it appeals to her whimsy their knowing each other.

Allie says to Francis, "Why aren't you with Jess?"

Frances smiles an apology to Jess's discomfort. Last time Allie left, Francis had not wanted Jess, not then and not now.

"She knows the signs of wind and water ….. I'd have her."

Jess wants Allie, impossibly, ridiculously. Allie asks for another Bourbon in Bourbon mood. Jess watches the falling dark curves of her hair snatch the light just above her forehead. Her expansive look and their frail union.

***

Day; without Allie. Jess walks with the crocodile down to the estuaries high tide dawn. The crocodile lies, slivering, inching, splashing crocodile movement. Jess vexed weeps for Allie.

Allie's crocodile seeing comes towards him as comfort. Jess slices it belly over and cast-iron blood. He eats crocodile flesh gorgingly and leaves dispassionate, crab like eyes on a cast-iron head.

The Osprey of Fatty George

From the very first day he'd arrived in the town, they'd named him "Fatty George." He'd arrived on the public bus which crossed the low lingering summer green hills, across the estuary bridge to arrive in the town on the storm blustered straight. George is a large man, a massive man, the size of a Southern Wright whale, the ones stranded occasionally in the estuary mouth. The townspeople wondered how he managed to squeeze through the door of the bus, but he did, carrying a tiny suitcase and an overcoat. At the autumn edge of summer, the south coast weather is famed for it's dramatic changes. Fatty George came prepared. He has come to buy land on the Barwin marshes. He walks down the track to the marshes with the air of a Don Quixote, fixated on his dream, his vision, his inspiration. And like Don Quixote, he quickly becomes a point of mirth to the citizens of Fairhaven.

"He is going to buy land on the marshes!"

They snigger. No one buys land on the marshes, there is no land to buy, at best, right now, at the end of summer the water lies in channels four feet below the heath banks, but over winter and spring the waters swell until only a few islands of land remain above the dark, dank, swirling waters. Even now, the marshes are desolate, a grey-green, tumble of low heath, tea-tree and mangroves on the distant shore, a grey, grey brown, muddy water lapping green brown landscape, low, monotonous and as often as not covered in a thin, ragged mist.

Fatty George loves the marshes, they resemble, he says, the coast of Norfolk where he was born. He brought two lots of land situated on a rare portion of the marshes which didn't completely get inundated in winter and very, very slowly he began to build his house. He built it from wood, some new, some second hand and some salvaged after the squalls which constantly lash the coastline, all stored under a tattered tarpaulin for months and months, such that the wood slowly bleaches into the grey-brown hue of the marshes. As does Fatty George himself, in his great grey oil-skin coat, huddled near the transom of his green wooden dingy, George supplements his invalid pension both fishing and finding treasures in the waters. And George would have completely disappeared into his marshes if it wasn't for the arrival of Rebecca.

Rebecca is a thin girl, eleven or twelve years old with short brown hair and a small curious face. She has left the city after her mother's death to spend time with George, her mothers brother. She arrives alone on the bus, wearing a red dress far too big for her, a blue cardigan, embroidered with the white flowers she likes, and carrying an old, and much used, suitcase. George waited at Forester's corner, he waits beside the stone war memorial, at the centre of the round-a-bout where the bus will stop. A cold wind sweeps in off Bass Straight. George regrets that he has come without his coat. On the marshes, you don't have the same wind as the town, and while it is dank, it is also warmer. George hadn't expected it to be this cold.

The bus arrives. Rebecca alights. She smiles warmly when she sees George, whether out of relief or delight is hard to know. The wind lifts her hair and wraps her red dress around her legs, she wraps her thin arms around the massive bulk of George, not quite around, not even half. On George's face, a smile blooms.

"Was the bus ride okay?"

"It's a little bit scary around the marshes."

George laughs.

"It isn't scary, it is beautiful."

"It's misty."

"Yes," says George, "Sometimes it is misty."

"Come," he says to Rebecca, "I am going to show you the beauty of the marshes."

They walk down the road from Forester's corner to the marshes watched by the townsfolk who wonder just who the young girl is? Is she his daughter, or more likely his niece? And why has she come, it isn't school holidays, and where is her mother? They feel sorry for her having to stay with Fatty George on the horrid marshes.

"Do you really live on the marshes?" Rebecca asks George, as they descend the steep hill of the town rise towards the track through the marshes.

"Yes.'

"Are there ghosts?" she asks, her eyes wide with wonder.

"No."

"You don't have to lie," says Rebecca very seriously, "I have nothing against ghosts so long as they are my size."

"There aren't any ghosts," says George.

What there is; is a little green house with red windows and doors, a vegetable garden slightly over-run with blue flowering borage over which cabbage moths flutter, germaniums growing in old paint pots and a small wooden boat which Rebecca likes, "can I use it?"

"If you learn the ways of the marshes."

The marshes are flat, non-distinct grey green which merges into brown green estuary waters. Rebecca's room is olive green, she has grand windows, at least in her eyes, looking over the water all the way to the mangroves and house roofs of a distant shore. And if you sit very quietly, which she often does, you can hear the rolling ocean waves crashing on the estuary sand-bar, where she and George will walk to and where she found the pale green sea washed bottle which becomes a vase for the tiny white flowers she gathers in the marshes, in memory of her mother.

Every morning, as a soggy, mist shielded sun rises from a mangrove shore, George prepares breakfast for himself and Rebecca, toast and sausages, an English breakfast. He whistles old music hall tunes from another time and another place. He smiles at Rebecca who is becoming increasingly sad.

"You don't like the sausages?"

"I like the sausages"

"You don't like the marshes?"

"No, I really like the marshes."

"Even if there aren't any ghosts?"

"Only little kids believe in ghosts."

"Then why are you sad?"

"I don't like school."

"But if that is so how will you learn?"

"What do I need to learn?"

"To read."

"I can read."

George doesn't know what to say about school, only that she must go, which he tells her. He doesn't like to say it. He can see that school makes her nervous and sad and he hates to see her like that. What Rebecca doesn't tell George is the real reason she doesn't like school and it is not because she doesn't want to learn, rather that she doesn't want to learn about the one thing school teaches her and that is what the town thinks about Fatty George. They say, he is a miser. They say, he is mad. They say, he is untrustworthy, and they say, that if anything sinister happened at Fairhaven, Fatty George would be solely responsible. Except that nothing ever happens at Fairhaven, not only nothing sinister, but nothing at all.

It is a resort town, whose fashion has passed, the residents maintain their old family guesthouses, their billiard rooms and their tea rooms for their rare clients, they try to take care of their gardens and stop the plaster from crumbling onto the billiard room tables. There are more people on pensions than people who work, including George and all the young folk are going away. The billiard rooms still open, the tea room as well, Forester's store's always been there and they guess forever will. But they know there are less people, less tourists each year. And no one has settled since the day that George came.

He is not one of them, he doesn't join in. He doesn't go to the old white church on the hill beneath the great green Norfolk Pines, every Sunday. He doesn't go each Saturday to the Barwon Bridge Pub to talk with the men about how the team fares (Badly, they might have to merge) and talk of games passed, those long-ago games, when they were champions, when they were great. And he doesn't stand on Saturday morning outside Forester's store to gossip about things, mostly about him, and the girl, the strange girl who came. What is it about the girl? Where does she come from? To whom does she belong? There is something strange about the man and the girl and their co-habitation. If George had been slender, he may have gone unnoticed, but a fat man cannot disappear. He is a landmark.

Rebecca dawdles to school or simply doesn't go at all. She goes as far as the corner and then follows the sea cliffs or returns to the marshes exploring where the heath is a tapestry of flowers or to the few places where it is cushion soft to lay upon and look at the clouds buffering across the sky, white and ballooned as sailing ship sails. She tries not to go too far, only a little along the cliff face to watch the ocean birds white and immaculate flight circling the fish below before their violent precision dives. Sometimes she finds crabs in the rock pools below the sea cliffs, or watches the mud crabs on the estuary scampering across the mud banks back to the channel. She tells George some things and not others, but only on the condition that he promises to explore new places with her. About other discoveries she is mute, they are her secrets.

"I saw the estuary from the school today" she tells him excitedly, "It was so ruffelly."

The estuary is never really rough, but the waves can be dangerous, short, choppy and abrupt. They can toss and sway a little wooden boat. They can play and swamp it. It makes Rebecca fret for George in his fishing boat. She isn't capable of concentrating when the wind blows and the wind blows more violently on the cape where the school house is than down on the estuary, which exaggerates her anxiety. And when the school day is finally over, when the school bells have finally rung, she returns home flying down the track from the cliff ops.

"You will take off if you run too fast." George says as she runs towards him.

"Really, truly," Oh if only she could, she wishes as he says it.

Then she asks George very seriously, "How was the estuary today?"

"Choppy," he says, then he smiles to ease Rebecca's anxieties, but he doesn't.

She knows his boat is very sturdy but the wind still fills her with disquiet. Later in the evening, when the wind has stilled, they walk down to the to the estuary over the duck board planks which George has constructed to cross the low lying coastal heath and squishing mud of the estuary banks. The sun is setting, the wind exhausted, the light a still brown with light mist descending.

"Tomorrow will be calm," says Rebecca.

"Perhaps," says George.

"Is the estuary always like this, so temperamental?"

"I suppose so."

"And the crabs, have they always been here.'

The mud crabs scamper across the mud beneath their haphazard jetty planks. Rebecca loves the mud crabs, their frenzy, their multitudes.

"I don't know much about the crabs, maybe you'll learn about them in school."

"No," says Rebecca and looks sadly towards George. then adds, "You are a panda, big and wobbly."

"And you are an eagle the way you soared down the track from school."

They take a long walk in the late autumn light. the mist low and lingering, George telling Rebecca that he believes the world can be generous. He had come here to live on the marshes like the fishermen of Norfolk who he'd always watched, going and returning in their shallow wooden boats with their white sails flapping. They would go to sea, he tells her, to catch bream, mullet, and herring, they would go to sea like heroes. Rebecca dreams often of such a boat with it's white sails in the wind, but she doesn't believe what George believes, about the generosity of the world.

"Yes," says Rebecca, "You should have a boat like that, but how is it possible?"

"It is possible," affirms George.

***

In winter, the river floods. Their Wellington boots sink into the water, despite George's duckboards. Rebecca leaps from tussock grass to tussock grass but once a day at least she slivers and slides off her landing into black and squishy water. Meanwhile the townsfolk are beginning afresh with a new set of rumours they have made up themselves, rumours about her mother, rumours about her and malicious gossip all about George. Rebecca sits in class and pretends she is not, dreams that the floods could cut their house off, from the school and the town and never go down, dreams they would leave them alone for a while.

Every day, after eating her English breakfast, prepared by George and after helping George take his nets down to their rickety jetty, and after they have discussed, seriously, the best places to fish that morning, Rebecca will return slowly to the house, where she will gather her school things. To go or got to go? It becomes harder everyday. As she climbs the hill to the school house she watches the ospreys glide on the sea breeze, over the estuary, searching for food. She dreams, she knows all that they know, about the currents and channels and fish, if she had their eyes she could tell George to go, this way or that way on the mud brown lake.

In the evening, she tells George how she watched the ospreys this morning, searching for fish.

"And where did they find some?"

"Towards the old wharfs."

"Then that's where I'll fish tomorrow."

The next morning George sails towards the old estuary wharf, the old put-put motor staining along. Rebecca watches the osprey fishing again amongst the old pylons of the estuary quay. She says to herself, it will all be okay as she climbs in the direction of the old red brick school, believing that maybe George isn't wrong about the world being generous, but no she says, "Nah!"

The rumours now say how George has kidnapped her, that she comes from the other bank of the estuary, from a house behind the mangroves where her mother weeps while Fatty George refuses to bring her daughter back, presumably in his old wooden boat. The older kids speak of things which she doesn't understand but hint of things more horrid than she can imagine. After lunch Rebecca leaves school, quickly climbs the hill leading to the cliff face and equally quickly descends to the cliffs, where the osprey soar above the estuary, sqwarking and squabbling amongst themselves as they ride the winds. Rebecca watches them all afternoon, observing their fishing techniques, the way they flick and twist their wing feathers in subtle and constant maneuvering and listens to their incessant cries as they leave and return to their nests.

Later in the evening George tells Rebecca what he caught near the old quay where the osprey were fishing, mostly mullet but a good catch. Then he'd asked where she'd seen the osprey this afternoon.

"They were fishing close to their nests near the estuary cliffs."

And he'd asked her if it was as good for her at school today as it was for him in the fishing boat.

"I don't like school." she said in a tone which closed the conversation.

So, they talk about the boat with the white sails and the ocean beyond the estuary, so deep blue and deep. And George tells Rebecca about the winds, those that come off the shore and those that come off the sea and the trade winds which eclipse them all.

"It will be okay," says Rebecca, but says it for George, because it won't be, she knows it won't be, not if they stay in this town.

***

It is the weekend and for two days Rebecca can accompany George. These are the best days, the best of times. There is a light hazy mist, sunlight saturated with dew and on the distant trees of the far bank a twinkle of sunlight reflected. The boat an effervescence of water beneath the bow and the put, put, put of the old Seagull outboard, and then the motor's cut and the still, silent calm of the estuary. A slight, slap, slap, slap of the waves against the sides, the first call of the sea-birds, the gulls, the terns and the osprey, highest of them all, flying in ever diminishing circles. Watching, watching, then darting towards the sea in one long magnificent dive.

"There are fish," says Rebecca.

"Yes, there are fish."

They bring in the net slowly until it reaches their jetty and then slowly sort out the fish, putting the saleable fish into George's big cooler, which they will take to the co-operative. Clouds gather on the horizon and a grey rain begins to fall on the darkening marshes.

**

Rebecca looks at the landscape from her bedroom window, headlights turned on prematurely on the estuary bridge, lightning on the ocean. She waits until he is finished and comes to eat his hearty potato and leak soup, talking of the sea and of Norfolk. And already the weekend is over, Rebecca is stretched out on her bed, listening to the wind blowing strongly from the west, tomorrow will be choppy on the estuary and even worse at school.

The next morning, she is tired and tense. George should not go out today, but he does, walking stoically down the path to the jetty and launching the old green wooden boat into the water. Rebecca watches him from the jetty, she wants both to go with him and for him not to go. As she returns to the house she decides not to go to school, not today or ever again, she goes instead to the bluff where the osprey are riding the wind currents, spinning then climbing again. They cry, their high-pitched chirp to each other while gliding above the water. And an idea slowly forms in Rebecca's imagination; if she could just wish herself into an osprey's body she could both protect George and escape the pettiness of school. All she'd need to do is wish, wish from the places where wishes are granted, wish from the places beneath, the bottom of her heart. And she wishes it, wishes the feathers which sprout from her arms, as if she were putting on a garment, no, a skin, and her beak, like a carnival mask, but strangest of all, so strange it amazes, are the eyes, it is as if she had binoculars inside her head. She can see the little landing jetty which George has built at the bottom of their yard. She can see George pull in nets in the estuary channel, his brow creasing with the effort and she even sees the little green vase and its fresh white flowers behind her bedroom window. And then there is the first flight, a terrifying leap of faith, but very soon she adapts, she has watched the osprey she knows how they do it, how they soar and spin, how they adjust their wind feathers in the slightest of tilts, constantly checking, adjusting, a tiny flick here, a tiny flick there. Rebecca soars, rises, spins, swoops how extraordinarily beautiful to fly through the air. High above the channels, the sandbars, the reefs and the schools of fish darting like arrows below.

Rebecca begins a descent and lands on George's boat's bow.

"Hallo Osprey," He says.

"Hallo George." Replies the osprey.

George face turns ashen, fearful and distraught.

"It's me!" says the Osprey, "It's Rebecca, your girl."

"But Rebecca's a little girl," says George.

"I'm disguised," Rebecca replies.

"Why?"

"Because I have to."

"Oh," says George, then he thinks for a moment, "Have you seen any fish?"

"I see everything, the fish, the channels, the mud banks and the sand bars."

"Good," George says.

After returning to the jetty and pulling in the net through the choppy waters, George asks the only question which troubles him, "You aren't going to be an osprey forever?"

"No, it's only a disguise silly, I can be myself again anytime I wish," (Hard enough) she said, only to herself.

The next morning Rebecca pecks at the sausages George has prepared for her in a troubling bird like way, before flying in front of the boat guiding George towards the most fish full parts of the estuary. And although he has never made such good catches, he is deeply troubled by her metamorphosis, she's just not the same. Even in the evening, as they chat in the kitchen beside the old wood burning stove when Rebecca returns to her little girl form, there is still something birdlike in the twist of her mouth, in the way her head tilts and the depth of her eyes, the osprey is present, and each day it grows worse.

And even though George is catching more and more fish it is comes at the cost of Rebecca's retreat before the strength of the eagle, who won't be denied. Rebecca no longer talks like they had about the marshes or even the fishing boat with its glorious white sail. She only speaks now of the wind and the sky, of flying and soaring and her life on the air. George fears he hasn't much time to lose, that he must do something and it has to be now. But what, it's a mystery, he hasn't a clue.

It was the very last day that she spoke, that began, what he knew was simply a desperate plan. She just sat near the window and stared at the night at passing dark clouds and a sliver of moon.

He knew the plan stupid, he knew the plan daft, but if he aimed very carefully he could shoot off her wings. For an osprey without flight isn't an osprey at all, if he could ground her, she would come back a girl. She wouldn't be lost to the eagles and sky.

He thinks all night about his plan, not sleeping a wink and crying inside. But in the morning Rebecca's wilder and further away, it's just now or never, whatever he thinks. He takes his gun quietly and hides it beneath his fishing nets, fishing bag and all his boat things. That morning she flies higher than usual making sinister cries above the wild marshland heath.

He knows he can't do it and knows that he must, not today he can't do it, it's too much to ask.

The next day, she is more wary, she senses George's fear. She leads him to the places where the most fish gather but instead of perching on the bow of his dinghy to watch him fish, as is her habit, she flies in tight circles far far above him, too far to shoot.

And so, it's the next day as she begins her ascent he raises his weapon and prays to his God. Bang, Bang the gun resonates, over the waters and over the heath, and she falls, like a little girl, falls from the sky.

"I've killed her!" cries George to the marshes he loves. "I've killed her, I've killed her" and the rows the boat over to the place where she fell. She lies on the tussocks in one of her secret places. George kneels beside her and lifts the girl up. Her arm, oh so human, is bleeding and sprained, he lifts her so gently into his boat looks at the girl he has rescued, he thinks, observes her small body, so fragile and thin, he red hair is ruffled, her breathing is taunt and sees the small changes, the beginning, he knows of the woman she's becoming, that one metamorphosis that will change their whole world.

Rebecca looks at George. She smiles, a sad, defeated smile. There is no way, she thinks, no way for a girl to flee from this world.

STORIES OF THE
RED DESERT

A Fisherman and a Dragon Atoll

Cactus rows, splash, glide, splash and stroke an aluminium dinghy on the lake peppercorn dawn, pelicans row, sleek bodies, ungainly beaks. The lake is an overflow from the Great Anna Branch of the Darling River into low sand savannah, except for a few holes it is shallow and will evaporate quickly; now the white days are beginning. What Cactus notices - everytime he catches a fish, the lake drops, yesterday it dropped a metre of it's radius for ten cod and six perch, the day before, half a metre for twelve perch, (it does not drop for uneatable carp.) And it is not when he hooks the fish but when he knives them gill to gill that the lake drops.

Sorrel would not like to hear this - always she says to Cactus, "I don't like this fishing there is plenty of work on the vines."

His wife does not understand, he has finished with the vines, matting lines across the sun, against the sun. And Cactus doesn't understand this Sorrel, with the jealousy of his fishing and of the savannah. He does not love this Sorrel who wishes him to make the more money on the vines, but the Sorrel of the dicotyledon Blackwood hills who was tall and slim with low hair tied down her back and silk muscles falling as a newsreel animal - more like an antelope than zebra or giraffe. He took her to Sydney, where one Sunday they almost incidentally came to Green's Park (He thought of an old friend's name.) That day, for no great reason, did not grow obstinate like some. They spent it sitting, talking in Green's Park. Somewhere a guitar played as unobtrusively as a cicada and that night with the best of friends, after the best with each other.

Once again in Sydney, the morning of a night's sleepless truck ride, when he'd walked up William street where a fire hydrant had gushed water through the early morning washing the gutters and giving that small bit of city a fresh vacant smell like thunder coming and he found Sorrel, not at Victoria Street but a Darlinghurst Street and not until the afternoon when the city was sick. Cactus didn't know, still doesn't know if that was a betrayal. He cannot dissolve those uncertainties lying just under her expressions as carp squirting mouths across the lake.

Cactus hooks something, a cod. He pulls his line in slowly, sculls the dingy directly over it. The cod will move when it tires of pulling against him and it will move up - there are no deeper holes to sink into. Cactus cannot pull directly against the cod, it may be heavier than his lines break of fifteen kilograms - this break is a certainty. Cactus keeps his line taut and waits. the cod moves, he reels in more line and sculls the dingy directly over it. Again, it moves, again reeled in, again and again, until Cactus sees it red finned, red bodied swipe against the surface. Cactus has his quill net ready, the cod snared within it.

He knives it gill to gill; the lake drops. He catches a Murray perch and another two cod, this is good, even though the lake drops. He has caught enough to pay for today and quieten Sorrel's dislike of his fishing. Some days he doesn't catch enough to pay for the day - these are bad days, other days he catches more to compensate.

At the first vineyard town, there is what looks like an old Shell petrol station, but instead of the petrol sign it has one saying, "Fish & Rabbits Brought". Here Cactus sells his fish. Only sometimes Cactus takes back Murray Perch to eat for Sorrel doesn't like fish. Sometimes Cactus thinks there are fish worth more than perch or cod, but this is a stupid thought - it is like Sorrel buying tickets in the lottery.

Now things aren't going as well, the water has fallen again and only carp are being caught. Cactus tries all the holes of the lake but only carp are hooked. Yesterday he caught carp, today nothing. Sorrel watches him eat the sandwiches she has made for him and drink the tea. Cactus says nothing; she is angry.

"You didn't catch any fish."

"No."

"Why?"

"I didn't catch any, you can't catch fish everyday."

"You didn't catch any yesterday either, maybe you won't catch any tomorrow."

"I'll catch some tomorrow."

"Sure."

"Yep."

He caught carp.

"You didn't catch any fish today."

"I caught carp."

"You can't sell carp. You may as well catch nothing as catch carp."

"I caught something, I haven't lost me luck."

And he hadn't lost his luck. The next day a perch is hooked. It fights a perch fight but Cactus concentrates his desperation onto that taut line, the perch is taken and the lake drops. Another perch is hooked, another drop of lake. This day and the nest day Cactus catches Murray Perch, Sorrel is pleased with the money and the lake drops. On the third day of his luck, he catches only one perch but with it's drop of lake, the carp desert the water - all the carp, flapping on the banks like fishy mangroves suffocating in air - for this is the carp radius of lake.

"You caught nothing today."

"I caught a perch."

"One perch is not enough….. I don't like this fishing."

Cactus says nothing to Sorrel about the lake shrinking and the carp deserting it. It is a limit that troubles Cactus (as Sorrel troubles him but in another unfathomable way) could it be the limit of fishing or only of carp? He watches out the caravan door, prickly pear and grape pickers in afternoon heat, moving slowly with bent backs, tattered hats crawling down exhausted vines. Sorrel was not always like this, she did not always have this want of money, it grew into her with the viciousness of that frog-faced man, her father, who in Blackwood hills (He knew) told Cactus, that Cactus knew nothing, never would. Was good for nothing, never would be. It is this callousness that makes that family hurt him, trying for their wants.

Sorrel watches Cactus looking glum.

"You should work back on the vines; this fishing is not going well."

Cactus nods, it is true of course. He says very little this night. And sleep brings a strange phosphorescent ocean, his fishing lines plummeting the same twine streak as light rays on the lee side on an island - an atoll;

a transparent spirit atoll with storms, thunderless, weightless and vines hanging knots in the air.

There is little lake for Cactus to fish, into what is left he casts disinterested loop-a-loops of line and waits watching above him, wedge tail eagles sailing wide slow flapless turns. They are hunting the drying out savannah for shingleback, dragon lizards and plague rabbits. And the sheep have come down to the lake boxwood trees, they will eat out the wallaby grass as far as a day's walk, as far as a cockatoo's flight (his mornings alarm with their flight disturbance squawks). Everytime Cactus catches a fish, he tightens the web of savannah, of hunter and hunted, thirst and charity, for fishing is magic - not a happiness magic - but one that casts more meshes of debt, and yet nothing hunts a man.

A line jolts, Cactus reels it in cod taut. He pulls it in as tight as he dare and the line twings across the water. Cactus lays the line over the bow of the dingy, angled away from the cod in a rising and nervous north wind. The cod moves; because of the wind? An air on edge and a ground evaporating into a dust filled sky. The cod will not act truly while it blows. The cod strikes the surface, quickly, unnaturally. Cactus sees its fin cutting red in the red air. He reels out more line, the wind whips it up and tows on the dinghy. The cod moves towards him across the hoarse lake to confront and to lose - it must lose against man and quill-net. And when it has lost, when it is tangled in the quill net, knived gill to gill, the lake quietens, sounds a long low screech, a whirlpool roar grows in the lakes centre sucking water and dust into the earth, leaving Cactus and cod on a white acrylic land.

And tonight, when the cockatoos land on the water-less lake, they will die.

And tonight, when Cactus and Sorrel eat this cod, for Cactus will eat this last fish, he will eat it with great longing.

This night is too hot to sit inside the caravan, so they eat the cod with lemon and bread on a rug on the ground. Cactus drinks a bottle of Southwark beer. Vines and frangipani are acid and tang under a night so firm with stars it might sink them.

"You will go back to work on the vines?"

"Yes."

"I am not sorry that the lake should dry up."

"I am sorry."

"I did not like this fishing."

"No…… you did not.….. but until the end, I caught a lot of fish."

Cactus lies against the cooler-than-air ground. The lake's vanishing has left a hollow in his thoughts and a slow osmosis is beginning; of working the vines and Sorrel's wants and the black starlit night begins filling it.

"Most of those stars aren't stars," Cactus says to Cactus, "but rocks and junk in space."

Sorrel looks strangely at Cactus, trying to let nonsense fill his hollow.

"Do you think you'll make much money on the vines."

Cactus thinks that he won't, at least no more than the better fishing days, but says instead, "I'll make more than before."

"When you make the money, we should go somewhere else, somewhere far away from these vines in the desert."

She has these wants, they rise inside her, like carp, one after another, casually at first, then obsessively and nothing Cactus can do can quell them.

He thinks of the island of his dreams and the islands up north that are like that and thinks he could take Sorrel there; then that thought stings, the Darlinghurst Road, the morning the city smelt of thunder sting, which Sorrel doesn't know about, which Cactus keeps sealed like phosphorous in his soul. And Cactus says nothing about the islands up north as Sorrel's hair touches his leg, cooler than the ground.

Latter than the fishing time in a morning spray of light Cactus starts the truck for where he'll work the vines. He drives the long road that turns to savannah at the corner of prickly pear. At prickly pear Cactus brakes; he begins to wonder - if the water could not have returned to the lake in reverse of it's vanishing, sucked like salt to the skin of savannah. And whether he shouldn't go to the lake to see if it hadn't. He could start on the vines any day.

Cactus turns the prickly pear corner to savannah, out to the dust tracks to the thorn country. A corrugated track he drives too fast across, saltbush plains, belah rises and down to the boxwood rim of the lake. And where the lake was yesterday, today is a strange sight - for the cockatoos who last night came down to the lake to drink have died and over their bodies wedge tail eagles, gold goannas and red dragon lizards, snap and peck at dead cockatoo and each other, in a circus of eating.

Cactus watches passively this waterless lake which cannot free him from the vines he should've finished with and a hot banded sun also watches. These hungrier than clever lizards have forgotten the sun and that on this lake there is no shade even for something as small as a shingleback. The sun will do its own killing.

Some lizards scuffle off the lakes salt surface, some linger and the hotter and hotter sun preys on them. Cactus sees an older, larger bearded dragon. He is curious of this ancient animal lying exhausted on sand and salt near the centre of the lake. He walks over to it, it lies, a fragile metallic leaf body breathing quick heart strokes. Gold bodied, gold thorned and black opal eyes. Cactus has never seen an animal with such beauty as this. He wants to fish it, and although he could pick it up now he goes back to the truck for the quill net for he doesn't want to grab that thorn bristled body on the closed edge of death. And when the quill net strikes the lizard, the lizard dies, and when Cactus lifts it, it is metal, gold skinned, gold thorn'd and black opal eyes.

Cactus shows the beautiful metal lizard to Sorrel, hesitantly, restlessly, for Cactus has made the mistake of trusting men. The fish-buyer, who didn't know what this animal was either but showed the same electric emotion.

Sorrel says, "It is worth much… you must sell it."

Cactus does not want to sell it, it is his, it is the lakes gift.

He nods, "No."

And Sorrel is angry, "You must sell it, for us to go somewhere else."

Cactus looks at Sorrel - they do not need this selling to go somewhere else, but perhaps they should go, Cactus thinks and says this. He starts to pack the truck but Sorrel stops him, she wants him to clean out the smell of fish which she says, nauseates her. It is when Cactus is cleaning out the smell of fish that the Bullock appears. He appears by the caravan door, he is larger than Cactus, he is a bullock, with bullock folds of neck and chin mix. He comes from the Anna Branch where men look like this and he is hunting Cactus.

"You the bloke they call Cactus?"

Cactus nods he is.

"You found something on me land."

"I caught some fish on the lake."

"It ain't fish I heard."

The Bullock leans against Cactus in a way which threatens weight, in a way that a Bullock will fight. A fist strikes Cactus, the Bullock cocks Cactus's arm up his back.

Cactus says, "It's in the truck."

The Bullock, with Cactus's arm still pinned up his back forages in the truck. Sorrel is fearful, and furious, at cactus who should have sold it, at the Bullock for his thieving. She leaps from the caravan with a knife which she steers under the Bullock's abdomen. The Bullock lets go of Cactus and turns, the knife again. He drops in pain, blood stains his shirt creeping down the patchwork of his stomach.

Cactus grabs Sorrel, pushes her into the truck, starts it and drives over the only roads he knows away from the Bullock and the caravan, away from the quill nets of men, to the lake the Bullock cannot own and which has its own reckoning.

This night they camp on the lake. Cactus is certain they will hunt he and Sorrel. No, he is more than certain, relieved, that something will hunt a man. That debts he owes can be paid - he has taken over the kniving of the Bullock, it was after all always his, Sorrel only wanted. He sits near the lakes edge, the lizard near him, wrapped in a Sunraysia Daily newspaper. He unwraps it, wonders if it is still as beautiful as before. It has a gold body and veins of silver he hadn't notices before and black opal eyes which are like oceans at night with slight phosphorescent plankton. It is, if anything more beautiful. Cactus places it in front of him on the lake salt edge, as though it were still alive.

It is in the empty hours that the lizard grows brighter, grows fiery, illuminating Cactus and Sorrel sleeping beside him. It grows and grows, then leaps into the sky, a wedge tail or a meteor. The lizard's gold is sun, silver an atoll and deeper than ceramic blue, deeper and deeper the more Cactus looks into it, the ocean's opal swells. He wakes Sorrel to the atoll - and the reckoning of the lizard; his to be with her, and hers to be there.

Red Desert

"Across the red desert," says the man to the green lizard, "is the place lizards can fish in the sea."

"Lizards," says the lizard, "don't live in the sea."

"They do," says the man, "in the enchanted isles they call Galapagos."

There in far oceans laconic waves lizards scramble over algae's rocks, diving and fishing where waves flick and thunder. And like those lizards, says the man, the lizards of the red desert should go to the sea to fish rather than remain in this cannibal landscape, for the sea has fish aplenty and oh! so easily caught.

"What," asks the lizard, "will fish taste like?"

"Better, far better than eating each other."

"And what is the sea like?" asks the lizard of the man.

The sea is like the desert, except blue and green and the sea is lighter than desert sand, so light a lizard can rise and fall within it, but inside you must be certain not to breath, for inside is where anything but fish will drown. A lizard must breath at the surface and burrow down in holes which make themselves and rise again in other holes which also make themselves. And the sea is cooler than the desert, but always it is swift and so plentiful of fish.

"It is a strange place, the sea," says the green lizard to the man, "But perhaps it is a place where lizards should go."

One by one, then two by two, and finally race by race, the green lizards, then the red dragon lizards and reluctantly the grey geckos decide to journey with the man to the sea. They begin the journey, the man calls a diaspora, waiting under the verandah of the man's tumbling sandstone house while the man and the green lizard talk of the journey to the far and fickle sea.

"How," asks the lizard of the man, "do we get to the sea?"

"The sea is what the sun sets into."

"But lizards must travel by night."

"Then we will follow the stars which chase the sun, the zodiac stars, Scorpio and Virgo and tonight we will begin for the sea.'

In the scarlet evening the man and the lizards begin for the sea, across sandy dunes and sandy dales, over a moanish landscape, following the man who follows the zodiac to the Galapagos sea. All night long they seek the sea over each and every dune.

"How do we know when we reach the sea?" asks the green lizard of the man.

"By the sound."

"What sound has the sea?"

"It sounds as if it is breathing, and near the sea all birds are white, so even if we cannot hear its breath, we will see the sea-birds."

But not tonight or the next night do they hear the slow breathing sea or see the sea-birds, except in the imagination of some exhausted lizards. And lizard stomachs quake and creak as their hunger grows, for how can they hunt while they are journeying to the sea? On the third dawn a grey gecko collapses, seeing imaginary white sea-birds perched in the air, the red lizards scurry and snap at this their first meal since the beginning of this journey. The man is angry. The man is very angry, he yells at the red lizards, that when they reach the sea there will be fish aplenty, and there is no need to prey on each other again. Each night as they cross the red desert following the zodiac to the west, grey geckos die and the red and green lizards dine on their scanty kin. The man, although he is angry doesn't say anything, but hurries as fast as he can to the glint sea as vast and serpentine as the desert.

"What," asks the green lizard, "is this smell?"

"Fish," says the man of the salt and seaweed scent.

"Where are the fish?" asks the lizard looking over the filament sea, finding it fishless and so strange, for from afar, it is blue, but at it's skin it is clear.

"The fish are what you have to dive for."

"How," asks the green lizard, "do you dive for a fish?"

"By jumping head first into the sea, flicking your tail as hard as you can, except you must remember not to breath inside the sea."

The geckos first try diving from the algae'd rocks, crashing into the waves, flapping on the water and doing quite remarkable things to try and descend within. Eventually they do, to see but not reach some white-bait, so deep in the quirky sea that they flip out before they are near them. And the red dragon lizards swim with no more grace for their frill necks fizz in their dives twirling them into a mess of bubbles and tails. The green lizards, fools they are not, sit on the shore near the man and although a few slithers into the sea to look at the fish on the reefs, they know it is easier, so very much easier, to dine on tired geckos that night.

The man yells and yells at the green lizards in the gecko less dawn, telling them of the richness in the sea. Telling them that they need never eat another of their kin, all they need do is swim and dive and they can stay stomachful forever. Stomachful already, the green lizards lie lethargi-cally on the black rocks above the tide line watching the red dragon lizards practice their frilled necked dives which today take them skimming over the water to a smashing cartwheel end.

In the afternoon, the red dragon lizards finally achieve it, the perfect dive, the precise swish of their frills back into their bodies, the quick deep plummet into the clear fishing sea. They discover how to gauge the seas diffraction, how to drop straight to the fish below. Clever as cormorants they fly and fish with elegant ease.

"That is how to fish," says the man, "that is how it should be done."

And he asks the red lizards whether they breath inside the sea?

"No," they answer.

"Yes, that is how it is done."

"Does the water make its own burrow?"

"Yes," say the red lizards, "It does."

"As I said," says the man, "that is why they call the sea enchanted."

But the green lizards cannot skim across the sea, and although they find swimming easy, cousins to the Galapagos lizards as they are, it tires them more than scurrying across the red desert ever did. They sit on the black rocks and talk of the red desert behind the salt stung sea and at dusk they eat the red dragon lizards whose bellies are full of the strange taste of fish. At dawn, the man doesn't say anything, he sits at the waters edge and stares into the sea which only now begins its slow deep breath. The green lizards lie stomachs on the cool rocks above the salt spray gossiping about the red desert and every so often when the talk tires they tumble into the sea not bothering to fish. That night when their hunger returns, when there are no longer lizards to eat, the green lizards attack and eat the man who spoke only to lizards. They eat him little by little in their laconic way still talking of the red desert which the green lizards suddenly realize only the man knew how to return to, while haunting above them the first squawking sea eagle perches giant and hungry in the air.

The Desert of Gul Mahomet

*It was the Galah who sang the lament; the lament of the cameleer, a song
of his own invention and profound melancholy as only a Galah can know.
The Galah sang it shrilly, the Galah sang it sadly and the Galah sang it ad-
nauseum; from daybreak to dusk.*

*"We were the men who walked behind the heroes of the nation,
Dirty men in dirty robes with a train of camels
Bring me sugar, bring me flour, bring me,
all my needs and wants, bring me cameleers.*

*"Two mad Turks with guns explode, Bang! Bang!
Across the desert sands, Bang! Bang!
Were they villains, heroes, rogues or very, very stupid?"*

*We are the men you never see, the men you call the Afghans
men from Peshawar, Lahore, Punjab and maybe one from Kandahar,
We are the men you never knew, invisible men from desert camps
until the day, the Turks began, their battle of the desert."*

That was today.

Pre-dawn (Fajr)

On the first day, of the first year, of the first war of the world, in the
pre-dawn light of the last day of his life, Abdullah Aziz, recites the call to
prayer. The mosque is poor bush timber and corrugated iron, Ghan Town
is poor, this life is poor, and Abdullah Aziz is a bitter man. A deep mauve
sky, the colour of ribbons, the colour of mourning, slowly lightens over
the dust bleached hills, rocky, broken, granite outcrops, granite bones.

A red sliver of sun, split from the horizon, spliced by a dust haze over distant hills.

"God is great."

The desert scurries.

He has made his peace, at least with the desert, he will make his peace, the Peshawar way, today, peace with honour. A lead laden dust blows from the bullock heaps of the Silver City coating Ghan Town battleship grey. Ghan Town emerges in the dawn, a smattering of rammed earth hovels, on the edge of the desert, behind a slight rise from the Silver City, so as not to cause offence. Invisible, non-people of the Empire which brought us here with our camels, abandoned us here, if we return to Peshawar, we cannot return, we cannot see our families, we cannot bring our families to join us, we cannot ask to bring a wife, we cannot perform Hajj, as is our obligation, for we a muddled, dappled brown, are no longer members of this white man's land.

"God is Great," This they cannot take from me.

***

Abdullah Aziz has crossed this desert 172 times, it is a sandy desert, a scrubby desert, a rocky desert, and a silent desert. Abdullah Aziz resents that silence, the Prophet spoke to God in the desert, Abdullah spoke to Rasheed and eleven camels. Rasheed, from Kaza, a true Afghan, (they cannot be trusted) yet in his trust Abdullah lays his life. A cameleer's life, to crisscross this desert land, to cross the desert of stones, the desert of dunes, the desert of cliffs, the desert of sticks, the rust red desert, and the bone white desert. The white fellas gave them other names, names to honour, their great men, who cameleer's escorted.

Abdullah Aziz, did not want to hate, he knew where hatred ended. He was born the year the British came to quell the hot heads in his land. He came of age and they returned, to quell, and quell and quell again, his tempestuous people. Men in uniforms with guns, red coated soldiers, with polished boots, polished buttons down their coats, black felt caps and a way they looked at the native men beneath them. They offered Abdullah another life, an easy choice to make when they recruited men, with weapons drawn, become a cameleer.

In Australia, where is that? A long, long way from Peshawar. Abdullah Aziz, left his valley, left the high mountains, left his family, at the bequest of the British who wanted cameleers for the Empire and less hot heads on the frontier. Abdullah Aziz was not a hot head but he was a cameleer, and he knew the British red uniforms would be back, and back and back, because Peshawar men have great honour, and the British have none. Abdullah was escorted south to Lahore, Delhi, Bombay, Colombo, and Adelaide.

This land so foreign, oh so strange, so very hard to understand, no call to prayer from city spires, just bells which peel the hours away, no hawkers line the alleyways, just broad verandahs, bullock carts, coaches, horses, main street stores, white ladies under parasols, and harsh men in red uniforms. White man's cities, white man's rules for cameleers the desert.

They pioneered from here to there, from belah rise to gibber plain, from river bones to red salt lake, crusting, crystalline and sharp. This unforgiving desert land, crossed by dark skinned turbaned men who live on the fringes of their towns. The Silver City West Camel Camp, seventeen years and nothing more than a huddle of mud brick shacks.

"God is Great" The sun begins to rise above the desert hills.

Fajr (Dawn).

Each Dawn they resume this journey towards paradise, across the desert of prickly pear and Gul Mahomet wakes under a methylated moon from the lee side of a camel to find wood for the morning fire. For although this desert is bleak and the low thorny plants perilous, there are always some trees, or the bones of trees; mulga, belah, desert pine or sandalwood which Gul can burn. The galah, his self-appointed guide, squawks "good morning" to Gul rising from behind the camel, looking in similar directions for the likelihood of wood. Gul saying to himself and Galah - "Aziz should be here, awake to the camel's snores, to Galah's squawking and squawking." In this unreasoned caravan with the camel which is too slow and Galah, too talkative.

The old man Aziz was Gul's companion from the Afghan camp, a heaped bone gully above the Silver City of the Great South Land. Ironstone Aziz, with ship of moustache above his lip, stains of vein and cancer, and on his forehead a circle of hard skin the size of a half-penny, the mark of the prayer.

They would sit together around Aziz's belah fire, smoke hazing into low shaley, saltbush, quartz and needle wood ranges where camels trod slow foot-steps from their leases. After morning and evening prayer, sometimes talking, at others not, and at others simply being another in each other's lives. And Gul discovered the long harsh past of Aziz, where people and incidents stuck like architecture, here, there, at the twists and turns of his life that cannot be juggled fluid by if's; the past which lead to the prophet, while Gul's circled and weaved like a tailless kite.

Gul's story began in the village of Caaba, many miles distant from the great river, distant from the lands of rice and cotton, even the lands of wheat and long routes of date palms, a village in the poorest, desert twilight lands of spiny goats and scattered wheat. There were hills, far and small as a rise of dust - or, "are these Aziz's memories, his stories of his village?" Gul cannot picture whether these belong to Aziz or his own past, or if these are just the universal pasts of the Afghan Cameleers? He can picture the rock and bleached grey soil, the thorn bush fences which kept the goats from the crops, but now there are no hills, where have the hills gone? He would heard his goats into the badlands, along the transient creek wash-outs, sometimes as far as the village of Jacob's, or the village of Onar's, or the village of Nasser's, mud brick villages where the mosques were as poor as the Afghan Camp mosque. To pray in that slab iron mosque with its rock mihrab, after the great mosques of the Turkish city, blue as the Golden Horn, Aziz said, "is to taste our poverty." Khan travelled many miles with his goats, to places his brothers and uncles, who worked the fields, didn't know. Khan liked his travelling, place to place, field to field, he did not want to join his brothers and uncles, trapped in the village, to become as dull as his brother Abu, who knew nothing but wheat and date palms, who would sit with their father playing backgammon, talking of crops and the grey bone soil, which one day, on their death they would sink into and disappear forever.

So, when his father said, "In Kiamari there is much work."

Gul had already fled his village and he thought, it's poverty.

***

Gul Laughs at the desert, at the few small splintered mulga branches he has found. Galah laughs, probably at nothing. "So, small was my village, so little miles I travelled with my goats when I think of the oceans I have crossed. How little I must remember of my village Caaba, if the hills of Aziz's village I remember as my own?" Gul drags a few branches back to the snoozing camel and says as little his bad memory can recall of the salat, for Aziz of the Afghan Camp while he slaps warmth into his short khaki jacket.

"King on the day we are reckoned, show us the straight path."

Gul's fire has a little heat before an airless, inner-tube sun hatches the day.

***

A Tuesday, his last day in the village, and such importance in the day. Uncles and Cousins dressed as fine as for the mosque, came to their house across the dust square between thorn bush and giant green bougainvillea. They clasped and embraced him, which alone brought weight to the day. And his father sitting at the table of men, saying the prayers Aziz would say, eating goat meat and curry rice.

His father saying, "You must work hard, for in the city there is much laziness, and they might say, from the village of Caaba, come lazy sons, and do us dishonor."

"Gul Mahomet will not be a lazy son," said Khan's uncle, "not when he works for my brother-in-law, Rabal Khali."

Rabal Khali, the carpet merchant, for this is their decision, that Khan should work for this man in the city of Kamari.

81

"And you must pray in the great mosque and keep the holy days as Rabal Khali will."

His father, who said so little, said these things for the village, for honour, and not for Gul. It was a sadness of Gul's fleeing his poverty, that his father should not say the things which were meant for him, the things he'd imagined a father should say, about hope, and dreams, and respect. And Gul was glad when his father's attention shifted from him to the common talk of crops and where the salt was a problem, and how, if their poverty should vanish they could dig a drain from the oat crop to the low salt pans of the goat lands to siphon off this salt. How when Gul had earnt money in the city, he could help with this venture. He could come, although not in the holy months of Ramadan, to see this work. And Gul felt equally a man, who would work in the city for Rabal Khali, who would make the money for the salt drain, perhaps enough to buy some good land beside the stream. And on this day when Gul left his village for Kamari there wasn't any fear this dream could dispel - nor any truth to honour it.

***

Kamari was great mosques, minarets, motion and fear, it was humid and rotting and smelt like silage. And while there is great wealth, locked away behind high walls, Rabal Khali had none, nor any man he knew. And Kamari was the sea - taut and blue and steamboats resting on it like birds in the air, and every evening white dhows sailing the sea wind. On Fridays, after a week of the market and the quays, Gul and Rabal would kneel in the poor mosque, the devout Rabal reciting the Book, the dreaming Khan thinking of the grey-red rusting steamboats basking in the bay. The oh, so devout, and oh so poor Rabal, just like his father and his uncles and like Aziz, the quiet, quartz hardness of Aziz. And Khan could not say he ever knew Rabal Khali, nor his father and only sometimes he thought he knew Aziz.

***

"Did I know Aziz?" Gul asks himself, or Galah. Galah squawks and squawks as the sun slowly bloats, then begins to sing another of his pointless songs.

"Dark men dressed in swirling robes, on braying camels, here to there
Oodnadatta, Finke, Marree, and onto Wilparina,
the cameleers came and went, and then they disappeared,
Into their dust bound stinking camps, and prayed to foreign djins."

"Two Mad Turks with guns explode, Bang! Bang!
Across the desert sands, Bang! Bang!
Revenge is sweet, or bitter as a Hakea?"

"How useless you are Galah, you cannot think of another verse so you repeat this one over and over again."
And how disobedient is Galah, who will never seek the evenings water which is his purpose as a guide, and with the slow-witted camel, how little hope the caravan has of finding Paradise, even though they follow the direction of the qibla. How unlike the ships at sea, the paths of star and sextant, which though a mystery to Gul are eternity exact.

***

For Gul sailed from Kamari to the Southland, from the Southland to the Turkish city and from the Turkish city back to the Southland always seeking his fortune. Such journeys on ships called tramps but named individually, "Sovereign Star", the Greek "Hydra" and the Argentine "San Pablo," and even these, least amongst ships, small, red-rusting hulls of stinking heat, found in oceans, ports-of-call. Pitching, rolling, pushing, gliding, through the swells of the Southern Ocean, the doldrums of the Indian, and the droning hammer of the steam pistons, the haunting flat blue flatness of tropic sea. And now and again the seabird, albatross, tern and frigate bird, as fast as its name, devils of the sea, appearing, disappearing, without land to come from, or land to go to. These are the ocean journeys, slow, duplicate days, drowning in light, or blue, or enormous storms and the loneliness of foreign steamboats and even more foreign crews. And this is the desert journey, so equally duplicate, but so unjust, where is paradise? Aziz would know.

Abdullah Aziz is a man of pride, a man of honour and a man of God, he has made his peace with desert sand. In the desert a man survives, or doesn't. It's really very simple.

A pale men in uniform will come, again, again to the Afghan Camp, a man with reddish hair and a vicious grin, immaculate in desert heat, quoting law, not in the book, "The Silver City Abattoirs, Market and Cattle Sales Act." Cornelius Brosman was in charge of sanitation, nothing more. He didn't care that the Afghan Camp had a single well, that's all, no garbage disposal, no night man come, he only cared about one thing, to overlord the coloured men. To harass and sneer and laugh at the anguish he could bring. They are stubborn, unchristian men, who dressed in turbans, smelt like dust, who brayed to God's who don't exist, in foreign swirl of madness. A walking insult to Christian men, no better than their camels. They refuse to obey the laws, citing blasphemy as cause.

It is written, the Quran says, the correct way to slaughter goat, they would rather starve than eat, unblessed mutton, that's not bleed. "Let them starve", Brosman says, "it would solve one problem."

"I am nothing," Abdullah says, "If the white man takes my faith, law by law, and bit by bit, they have stripped us down to this. White Australia, go to hell, we are men with honour."

"We must clean this land of scum, we no longer need their camels."

Mid-Day (Zuhr)

They resume their journey after prayers are said.

They trudge slowly, at one or other angle to climb the steep dunes and over the dunes through hake and saltbush flats. Galah riding on the camel, the camel and Gul walking. There are no tracks, not even the animal tracks of the badlands, just red gibber rock, the rust cloud of tramp steamers, orange-yellow dunes and grey scrub, brown thorn bushes and the white tissue poverty of the Afghan camp.

***

When Gul first came to the Afghan camp, Aziz found Khan the occupation of Street Vendor, for unlike the other Afghans of the camp Khan was ignorant of the noble occupation of cameleer, journeying from outpost to outpost across the great deserts of this land. Aziz the Inam, and butcher in the Islamic way, painted an old wooden handcart, red and white in the swirling, puzzling designs of their way, and on a board above the cart, the words "Lakowsky's Delicious Ice-cream" in English, the same as Gul had seen on a shop in the Silver City. In the hot afternoons of spring and autumn, with the first and last dust filled winds of the northern desert and through the long intense summer, Gul would walk his cart around the circular paths of the Botanic Gardens - green as Kamari - a clattering whirl of wheels, bell ringing, he yelling "Ice-cream" in difficult English. And the wives and children of the miners, sometimes the white faced, deep eyed miners themselves would buy his ice-creams during green heat tempered promenades.

Gul would have to buy his stocks and ice from the pale British merchants who owned motor-cars and pushed their prices higher and higher. The same merchants who had once charged Abdullah for breakages which did not occur, for goods he did not know he carried. Abdullah would speak of these British, who owned the poverty in the Afghan Camp with great contempt. If he could, he would try to get his cum-uppance, he would never succeed. Mr. Bosman would arrive in the Afghan Camp in his neatly pressed grey-green uniform and his official, ru les an d re gula-tions, his vicious sneer and his contemptuous laugh, to harass Abdullah, because he can. And Gul had asked Abdullah, "Why have the British motor-cars and much wealth and the Muslim's nothing?"

Abdullah became very angry, for Gul is wrong, the British have nothing compared to the "Quran" and the Muslim everything because of his faith."

And Abdullah told him that the wealth of the infidel is Satan's wealth, as the motor-car is Satan's invention, and Gul would surely go to hell if he did not pray to stop these, heretical thoughts.

Gul did not pray to stop these thoughts, nor pray at all, and Gul did not tell Abdullah from this time what he truly thought, for Gul still wished for the British wealth and a motor-car, which he understood no more than the Quran. But even these were not Gul's greatest wish, Gul's greatest desire, Gul's greatest and most forlorn longing was for a wife and family. A dream which turned from hope to obsession, after he met the Irish girl Marree O'Connell, who brought ice-cream from him in the gardens and would smile and laugh with her thin acrobatic mouth. The girl with the freckled squat nose and eyes which hadn't any weight - like desert horizons - whose hair was mohair which would fall over her face so she would have to push it up over her forehead where it would hang for a moment then avalanche back.

And she would say things like, "My hair's a ratbag."

Which made Gul conscious of his own looks, he studied himself, his nose is too large and hooked, his skin and eyes are too dark, his face too thin and his hair too curly, and Gul could see why he could not find a wife. Even if Abdullah tells him the true reason was, the Afghan could no longer bring wife and family from home, only the white man has that privilege.

***

Galah thinks mirrors absurd, although he spends a great deal of time looking at himself.

"It makes me look like a bird," he squawked.

And Gul could not figure out what he expected. Although he should not expect this journey to make sense, and wished Galah would stop his ceaseless lament.

"What's the point of this desert? Where does it end?
Where does it go to? Where does it come?
What can a parrot know of these things?
Of someparrot paradise in squiggly words?"

Two mad Turks with guns explode, Bang! Bang!
Across the desert sands, Bang! Bang!
A life, a death, a tear, one for me and one for her."

***

Marree O'Connell would ask him, strange questions like, "Do you always sell ice-cream in the park."

When she knew the answer for she was usually there, perhaps Gul thought, this is a question only girls ask, for he knew very little about girls. There are very few women in the Afghan Camp, a few grandmas who'd arrived before the prohibition against coloured migration and a few women of the native camp who had married Afghan men.

"Yes," he'd answered, "I always sell ice-cream in the gardens and some-times I sell ice-cream in the Silver City itself."

She'd laughed at the name, "Silver City" as if it were a joke. And she would often let her ice-cream melt, because she was too busy talking. Always strawberry ice-cream, running down her fingers, falling knuckle to fine knuckle, a tiny river of pink.

"Your ice-cream melts," Gul would say as politely as his English could.

"Yes….. thank you," she'd answer with a startling smile.

Then she'd walk away across the gardens towards the miner's slums which surrounded the Silver City. She walked like an egret, long legs flowing forward her body follows, smoothly, beautifully. And when she'd gone some way from Gul she licks away the strawberry which had melted across he fingers.

***

That was the summer before the war, the last summer, before the talk of war began. All last year the rumours swirled, the Empire war, the war against the vicious Hun, the autumn war, the winter war, but certainly a war in spring. but not yet an Arab war, that was unexpected. The rumours swirled and flashed and boomed, like a distant desert sandstorm. Yet Gul Mohamed didn't know that it would soon engulf him. He knew his poverty and his hopelessness. he knew the bush timber corrugated iron dwellings of the Afghan Camp, the smoldering fires and the shaley quartz, goat dung ground. He knew the elegant buildings of the Silver City, ibis white in the deserts lithe light and he knew Marree O'Connell would be there in the Gardens, waiting. She would be standing under the trees tasseled light, in a red dress with small blue embroiled flowers, or sometimes in a yellow dress, as poor as Gul's grey work shirts, which she said embarrassed her. (The yellow dress, not the work shirts) And if they talked it would be about small things, how there day was, or what she liked, or hated, or thought ridiculous. She liked to talk about Ireland, where she came from, which was green with many rivers, she did not really like the desert which becalmed the Silver City in dust or harsh mid-summer heat and she did not like the mines which she said, took men's lives away. And curiously, she did not like the British, who had taken her Ireland away, and left them with their poverty. But mostly she liked to talk of the ridiculous things, of which Gul was one, with his Italian Ice-cream cart, painted she said, like a movable mosque.

And once, at the end of summer, when the sky was zinc, she'd asked him to come with her to the south silver mine pondage, where they could swim in the larger and clearest of the lead tallowed dams. Marree wearing the yellow dress which clasped her skin, and her hair was sprung black and wet after her long dives. She laughed at Gul, who couldn't swim, but stood knee deep, splashing arms and chest and face. Watching; Marree, bending and buckling through the water; and the boys who had erected a step-ladder deep in the water so only a foot or two surfaced, a platform to dive from, swimming around shoals of girls they were interested in and diving again; and the older men on the diagonal bank, drinking tan bottles of beer and watching the girls. And Marree touching his arms with her wet bone fingers and smiling so close to his mouth that their lips could touch.

***

They never touched and Marree was no longer always there, no longer there as long, no longer there as obviously. She tried to tell him what, in truth, he already knew, this world would never accept them, being together. And as the war grew closer, and the town grew tenser, what was unspoken that summer was more and more inevitable by autumn. They sent Marree O'Connell away. One day in March she wasn't there, and the next and the next. An old lady who had watched them many times in the park, told him, in a voice which bore both judgement and sympathy, that Marree had been sent to the Southern City. A hollowness descended on Gul Mahomed, a hollowness grander than the joy it replaced and Gul Mahomet knew the reason they had sent Marree O'Connell to the Southern City were the reasons Abdullah will say - above all, contempt for and hatred of, the Afghan men - the reasons they had betrayed the cameleers into such poverty, for Abdullah had been right in his despising the infidel and Gul had been ignorant.

Such an emptiness, Abdullah had spoken to Gul of this emptiness, this is the emptiness which men wish to flee through lust, through gambling, through drink, but whose only true solace is faith in the Prophet. In the time of their talking Gul Mahomet did not understand, either the emptiness, the solace, nor the Prophet, Abdullah said, he needed - his mercy, his paradise of gardens and rivers - to walk, to eat, to guide his camels across the badlands; no Gul Mahomet did not want this solace. He wanted revenge. Revenge for everything he felt, for everything that's been taken, and taken, and taken. Revenge to fill the hollow which feels like all the blood has drained from him, as the blood flows from the goats Abdullah butchers, after the hands have been washed to the elbows and the prayers read, after the blood has pumped, gush, stop, gush, into the desert sands, when the blood slowly begins to falter and the braying ceases, this is how Gul felt. And the thing he'd lost with Marree O'Connell, the thing he wished to have again, was the sweetness and the laughter and the hope.

***

Afternoon (Asr)

There is no hope. And there is no paradise. Just this endless desert and an insane Galah - singing from the back of the camel in the tightening heat.

"Marree O'Connell his one true love,
and now she has gone, she's gone away, not for her the quiet man,
who serves ice-cream in the park, a gentle word, a secret smile,
a gun explodes their dreams away."

"Two mad Turks with guns explode, Bang! Bang!
Across the desert sands, Bang! Bang!
This story can't end well."

Always Galah is useless, useless to ask anything of, useless are his rhymes. Perhaps he will find water, if his singing makes him thirsty, or if he becomes bored with his lament, or for the suction of sweat on Gul's back, or the eyelets of sweat, big as his eyes gently falling. But more likely in this desert where no place forward is preferable to any place past - except if there be water - Galah will do nothing bit sing loudly, uproariously and endlessly as an ocean.

***

As the oceans of his second crossings to the Arab lands - the tense ocean of cloud Himalayas, seas luminous as lighting and the engines beat enveloping the days - the longings and the disappointments of the Afghan Camp departed, and the wish to become a Turk in the Turkish land embraced. Gul, tense with these thoughts, through doldrum seas where monsoons bloat and thunder, through Mediterranean scattered squalls as the "Hydra" beats from the south. To the warm waters where sea birds swamp ports-of-call; Aden, land of the pilgrimage and the Quran - "Oh, that Abdullah should be here in the first days of Dhulhajja". Port Said, and then islands like mirages and squalls like islands, where sea and landfall, cloud and caique, disguise and mock each other. And even his first sight-ing of the great Turkish city is a trickery. It floats on the Sea of Marmara, moons of mosques and buildings stacked on buildings, stacked on air. Then it is real, a harbour like a night sea the sun cannot quite lift, the great mosques and buildings to the harbour where Gul found a room, neither clean or large, with bed and table and close enough to the old mosque to hear, breaking the day, the morning call to prayer, or in the evening, the calling from the minarets, high above the feverous, hurdy-gurdy of the great Turkish city.

But they did not call Gul Mahomet to pray, only to the city, to the great buildings which in this city, did not belong to the British, but to the Ottomans. They called him to the Spice Market, where storekeepers could understand little of Gul's bad Arabic, none of his good Urdu and much of his difficult English. Yet when he spoke English they grew uncomfortable with his speaking, even if it was about rice and dates like his village of Caaba and they would start conversations with people behind blinds or shop faces, who may or may not have been there in their Turkish tongue which Gul understood, not at all, because this man was wrong, and strange and different, he spoke English but plainly wasn't English, spoke Arabic incomprehensibly, perhaps he was Greek, he could be Greek but wisely didn't speak Greek. And whatever country he was from he was very plainly lost.

They called him to the harbour where he watched liners and dhows and great grey battleships, for more and more there are whispers of war. And to the house where women wear only stockings, where Gul lay next to the white waxy skin of these women. But they are not Marree O'Connell, these women had eyes closed and distant, not those eyes which felt like places transmarine - like the islands, mysterious as the sea birds in the ocean of his second crossing. Almost they called him inland where the villages must be, tattered crops of wheat and barley, olive grey of salt land and poverty in the hills as harsh as Galah's desert and as lamenting as his song of the wheat fields.

And finally, they called him to the great stone building where he could request to stay in this country; except Gul Mahomet could not become a Turkish man, because, as he discovered, he, being born in Caaba, is British, and while the Turkish people are not at this moment at war with the British, the British are in no way, their allies, and someone like Gul would be a perfect British spy, he, being a Muslim, he, speaking Arabic, and he being British. And, quite bluntly Turkey does not need another goat herder. (But for a certain sum - a sum Gul Mahomet did not have, could not obtain - history would have been different.)

"How could this be true, when my father farmed the Pescowie valleys and I was a goat herder, when I prayed with Rabal Khali the merchant in the poor mosque of Kamari and I lived with Abdullah in the Afghan Camp of the Silver City? How can this be true?" And they showed Gul the first map he had ever seen of the empire - "so many lands" - and they said, "This is why."

And although Gul did not believe he is British, nor this map, he did not understand how a map could lie. And if he were British, he knew, he ought not stay in the Turkish city. So, he began the third, and most purposeless crossing of the oceans, as hot and as useless as today.

But in his soul, he would not accept that he Gul Mahomet was British, for he, Gul Mahomet would die today under the Ottoman flag.

Dusk (Maghrib)

They stop under a cattle bush in a rip in a dune, Galah is in the bush pecking at seed capsules and dropping the hard wooden pericarp on the camel who is snoring swift sandstorms into the dune under his nose, twitching and braying when the pericarps land on his ears.

Galah sings,

*"Mr. Brosman, Mr. Brosman, hated in the town
hated in the Afghan Camp, hated, hated, round and round,
the man's a prick, he's nothing more than a turd in uniform,
let him pick on the Afghan men at least that keeps him out of town.*

*"Two mad Turks with guns explode, Bang! Bang!
Across the desert sands, Bang! Bang!
They should have killed that man."*

Over and over again.

Gul searches for wood in the cicada light for his rice and little meat he will cook in his round black bowl. And in the thin light there is a scampering, slivering and squawking as all the beings of the desert begin to join Galah's once solitary racket. Even Gul who recites the few words he can remember of the salat, "King on the day of reckoning, we ask you for help."

***

Gul Mahomet's return to the Afghan Camp was to the first time Abdullah was arrested. Mr. Brosman had ridden out to the Afghan Camp in his immaculate grey green Sanitary Officers uniform and dragged Abdullah back to the Silver City Courthouse, because he'd killed the goats on the flat ground below the Afghan Camp and not in the Silver City abattoir. "How could Abdullah kill in the abattoir, he is not a butcher, and how can we eat the abattoir meat when the prayers are not read and hands not washed to the elbows?" There was in Gul's return much confusion, confusion of war and confusion of faith. And Abdullah was fined in the British Court more than an Afghan can earn and no longer can Abdullah and any other Muslim have the goats killed in the Islamic way, or eat them killed in any other way.

Gul and Abdullah sat in Abdullah's mallee wood and tin rusted hut, talking of Abdullah's arrest, of the bastard Mr. Brosman and the war which had begun. And even though neither said so, both knew the other carried an equal hatred of the infidel, of their power over their lives and that the time of their disagreement had passed.

But they didn't yet know what that meant.

Nor would they know until Mr. Brosman came again and once again arrested Abdullah for slaughtering goats in the way which is written.

Abdullah says, "The infidel will war against us, it is what the Prophet says, we can only fight for the Prophet and hope for his mercy."

And although Gul did not wish to think of the Prophet, his mysteries or his mercy, he nodded surely to this.

**

Gul and Abdullah did not plan their ambush or did not plan it well. Abdullah knew a place where the annual New Years Day picnic train would steam a long slow curve out of the Silver City into the Barrier Range, to the mines and reservoir further west. And where a wooden trestled water pipe came down from the reservoir to follow the train track, that would be their fortress. Nor was there great fear in Gul, nor thought of death, only that the British had betrayed him into poverty, betrayed his love for Marree O'Connell; or if there was fear, it was, what would it look like, and how would it feel? What Abdullah thought Gul did not know, the ambush was one of the times Gul did not believe he knew Abdullah.

After dusk prayer Gul and Abdullah prepared the rifles the way Abdullah always prepared them before the old journeys into the desert. Abdullah cleaning his rifle, then showing Gul how to clean the older Martini-Henri rifle which curved under Gul's shoulder like a cripple. Then they wrapped their rifles in a hessian bag and placed them in the ice-cream boxes of the red and white ice-cream cart - Maree's movable mosque - and above the ice-cream sign flew the crescent and star flag of the Ottomans; a bout of reasons for their revenge on the Silver City in general and Mr. Brosman in particular. He would be on that train, in his crisp and despised grey-green uniform.

***

Gul slept fractions of that night, as this night, if he sleeps at all. "I sleep if I am to believe the stars movement across the sky but not if I am to believe the camel's snores of Galah's inane songs." Galah has eaten so many cattle bush nuts he cannot more from his branch, nor think of a song to sing over his cattle bush stomach.

***

Dawn, the call to prayer, the call to battle, the prayer of mercy and reckoning, on this day, the day of the ambush.

On the first day, of the first year, of the first war of the world, in the pre-dawn light of the last day of their lives, Abdullah Aziz, recites the call to prayer. Abdullah and Gul drag the ice-cream cart, one handle each over the bouldery goat track which skirts the Silver City, over the white rock outcrops and down to the water-pipe fortress. They lay on the ground beside the water pipe, rifles against their shoulders, eyes on the long curve of rail track below. Abdullah whispers the circular Arabic prayer of the goat killing, cleansed his hands and arms up to the elbow in desert sands. Sand ebbs in the slight wind which catches the Ottoman flag. Sand ebbies into Gul's eyes.

The train came slowly, streaming black and long and turning into the curve rising towards them. There are many fears, then a rifle fires beside him, a bullet cracks and another. Abdullah has seen the grey-green uniform of the Sanitation Officer, far and wee in the distance. He shoots again and again; the man falls and someone beside him. Gus fires as the

95

train stopped and a panic of people duck into the ore carriages and scatter behind it. And there was a man on a push bike beside the train. Gus fired a shot for Marree O'Connell, a shot for years of humiliation a shot against the powerlessness which has been his life. The man on the push bike fell as Abdullah took Gul's arm and signaled they run from the chaos they have unleashed. To the white rocks, quartz outcrops with a few struggling, marooned in desert heat Belah bushes, and here Gul's pain and fears overwhelm him, fears beyond this place and time, beyond his poverty and the Afghan Camp and beyond even the Silver City, distant and metallic in gun-shot light. The fears Abdullah had spoken of, that the world was about to vanish from Gul Mahomet, as it had from the push bike man, as it slowly seeped from Abdullah Aziz, and there were no antidotes to either his fear, or to the guilt of the fate of the push bike man; only that they would be tied together in his death, and the struts of Marree O'Connell of his poverty and humiliation - "so confused and so weak are these things, and yet so determinate." But also, there is the harshness of the rifle, the desert heat and the cracked and splintered outcrop.

Night (Isha)

And the harsh night of flaxen constellations of this unreasonable journey over a desert of prickly pear. And, "Why do I travel with a camel, so slow, and a Galah singing and chattering, such meaningless things."

"Two mad Turks with guns explode, Bang! Bang!
Across the desert sands, Bang! Bang!
They kill the wrong dam man, what a disappointment."

"They shot the wrong man, what a farce, what a disappointment,
Brosman wasn't on the train, this war has gone so badly,
I wonder, wonder all the time if Gul Mahomet will ever understand,
Marree O'Connell wasn't lost until the guns were blazing."

The stupid bird, he's got it wrong, Abdullah's first shot found the man, the hated man in uniform, the man who turned his live to hell. Is that what this is, my own hell? Gus Mahomet didn't know. No, he knows, "Its nothing more than a desert vast and wide before the gates of paradise. It's what Abdullah had always said, "You must know yourself to enter paradise, in the desert, you find yourself, there is nothing else but camel dung."

He said nothing about a parrot.

He should shoot that bloody parrot, Bang! Bang!
And then he'd find paradise amongst the sand.
Or, at least some quiet.

STORIES FROM THE
HILL COUNTRY

Morning Parrot Trees

They'd never walked with Fisher - no one ever had. They sit in the Narcissus Hut and watch him pack the smallest rucksack they have ever seen. He is going to Mount Ida; East and alone, carrying little and looking fierce. They look on a map of east and Ida, find nothing worth the difficulty of climb. Mount Ida is not as high as a west Mount Acropolis and they only climb the highest peaks; these half dozen walkers, grandfather to grandson.

The Grandfather asks, "What's up there?"

"Rocks and scrub."

It is true; Fisher grins it true. Fisher drags on his wet boots, ties laces tight and sodden around his ankles. He is going to Mount Ida to see the parrot trees - to see their flowers flying in wind gusts, carrying a hold of pollen in their strange ritual of fertilization. Fisher never says that; because he doesn't want anyone finding the parrot trees, because he doesn't really like many people.

The Grandfather who'd mapped out the journey to Mount Ida, at least in his head, has heard about Fisher. He has heard - Fisher charts fast and lone these lessor ridges for reasons never told and now ceremoniously never asked.

The Grandfather asks, "You coming back by St. Clair?

"No, coming back here.....it's too scrubby around the lake."

The Grandfather gestures agreement about the lake. "I'll ask anybody going east to look out for you."

Fisher's faces "thanks", he meant to carry both, no one ever goes east. Fisher lifts the smallest ever seen rucksack to his shoulders, stands boots on the slab wood floor to test a tightness of fit and walks from the hut to the Narcissus River crossing.

Fisher crosses the Narcissus River and onto Mount Ida's high west slopes where people aren't but parrot trees grow. It is not the first time or even the second that Fisher has climbed Mount Ida. He has seen the parrot trees; observed the red-green flower's flight fertilization, what he searches for this time are the rarest (the might exist) black or white flowers.

It is dawn and Fisher climbs in light sleet. There is a ridge to his right, cloud mist ebbs across; grey, grey-brown, grey-green. It is cold. He wears his woolen jumper inside his shirt, a warmer combination. His boots and ankles jolt from rocks to rocks and sleet soaked fen. To quarry any of the flowers - and Fisher can only guess, especially the rarest ones - you have to reach them just after dawn. He walks fast, known Fisher fast, carrying little and with his lone animal look - or almost alone, he carries a small walnut deep polished pipe in his right-hand shirt pocket, his contemplation and company. And parrot tree thoughts, that he might find the black flower, its colours rarest branches.

The sun rises and Fisher hunts, down from Mount Ida mist into snow gums, river's first motions from fen soaks and rock drip falls. he hunts down into thick scrub, he beats scratched through, from a plateau top descending into closed gullies, fern and fen, then thicker acacia, banksia intergrifolia, parrot trees.

A parrot tree flower buds, red-green, Fisher moves slower now, noiselessly as he can to a natural hide he has seen many times before - a gully ledge above a cluster of parrot trees, he'll squat in, watch in, wait in, his disturbance die.

The flowers crack through their wood pericarp, sprout large green petals, large as a hand and rice paper thin with a curve for catching gusts of wind. Green petalled, red stammered flowers perch on branches then fly papery parrot flight. They bud as ducks from a dam fly, in ones and hundreds. A flower lands near Fisher, it's petals tremble in slight gusts along the ledge. Then something happened which has never happened before, it's petals change colour from green to red. Fisher's eyes snare the red flower, thinking if it can change to red then maybe to black, the rarest of flowers he has climbed Mount Ida to find.

Fisher moves towards the flower, close and closer, a mist ebb gust drags the flower up the gully slope. Fisher scrambles after it, (to find what colours destination is) over Mount Ida's dolomite top line, the wind carries its red papery flight and down onto a further east tiers. Huon pines, lakes, fen, flowers don't fly to. Fisher follows it, far behind.

When Fisher reaches it, it is caught in a Huon pine branch before a large moraine lake. It is white and sings a wind recessed song, on and on, it sings the metre of the wind, then it flies from the line out over the lake. Grey, then black, far over the lake stretching with it.

Fisher is stranded in exhaustion. He falls rucksack and him below the Huon pine, breathing the pace of flight. Did it turn black? - his legs will not follow and it will be gone before he reached the lakes far shore. He says these two things and says, it was black, to a pipe company of smoke. (He brings the pipe out from his pocket and lights it against the flight wind.) The pipe burns and decides all things slowly. It says, in a wind skirmish of smoke - all things look black in the distance.

It is colder and too late to return to a less exposed Narcissus River snow gum camp. He will camp here; his pipe agrees but is troubled. Fisher pitches his tent to the Huon pine, tied to where the white parrot flower had webbed. He starts a small fire; dry wood is scarce and a long calf-aching walk to find. Fisher cooks rice and tea on the pine branches slow burn. The tea is warmth and pipe company up on Mount Ida with a black parrot tree flower and no one to look out for him, east. He sleeps, wakes, sleeps, dreaming black parrot petal wings. Smokes, pipe silent as he in cold sleet night, dull drizzle dawn that grows light through five slow bowls of tobacco.

The tent guy, Huon pine sing above the sound of the wind in his black petal arms. Fisher breaks a green pericarp of tent, black rice-paper arms crab out and he perches on the Huon pine - the tent peels away from the branch, like canvas. A wind gust lifts Fisher. He flies; black into dark morning over the lake. Fisher trails a rarest of all, black flower.

Possum Moon and Redwoods

He is young, wears a workman's grey woolen shirt, sweat and forest marked. He has been in the hills behind the town, now he is sitting in a bar near three other men. Rain falls outside: from the ocean, high evening rolls of cloud, black between mauve sky, thundering rain.

One of the three had asked, what he did, or what he'd been doing?

He says, "Watching a tree race, " His face litmus'd, "They reckon …… the biggest trees come from America….. Redwoods," He stressed it.

They slightly tilted lips upwards, a smile, a nod. They guessed so.

One, an American agrees, "I've seen them they're great trees."

A shift - automatic, even unintentional. The American and the forest bloke set just aside. A light built American who'd seen Redwoods, been to California from a Pennsylvanian born in town with friend and friend's father who drove. Over the mountains they had camped within to a final west coast camped beneath - "the greatest trees on God's earth."

The forest bloke turned, swirled his stool on one leg a length closer to the American.

"There are Redwoods growing up there in the hills. It's what they are racing …. against Tasmanian Blue Gums …… to see which is tallest."

The American looks strange at the forest bloke.

"In this country - they race trees?"

They race trees. Either side of the Aire River valley, water thrashing down the valley sheer to the ocean. Fifty years ago, the Redwood led by a foot and each year since bluffs and tactics have complicated. Early bluffs and double bluffs as each tree tries to trick the other into growing during high late frosts and springs harsh storms. Bluffs which sometimes worked and sometimes not; on trees waiting wary with each spring's subtle starter.

The lead is always small and difficult to gauge. Observers climb higher and higher up the valleys walls to see level across the tree heights. They'd passed two hundred feet last summer, the Blue Gums half a foot taller.

He'd camped in a forestry hut which leaked between slab roofing - he'd pitched a canvas fly across the rafters. Late winter storms preyed off rees, their winter colour, green and winter blue webbed a tense apparatus of race. He stood in boots with laces open like night - a depressed rain wait.

Trees wait - tactics invented for springs first change. A Blue Gum will bluff the lower Redwood; for two early days it will grow, and the Redwood will have to follow, on the third day it will stop and wait the river mist rising first true spring day. The Redwood waits it's most precise found spring signal - a faint urine salt smell from a lower warmer valley.

In oil-skin jacket he stands on the river bank, rain water swelled, watching a yabbie, red and orange brown camouflaged until it shovels unexpectedly fast up the river.

It rains, still and on.

New green buds on a Blue Gums highest branches.

A Redwood waits cautiously.

He climbs to a watching place that day seeing a Blue Gum growing. The next day and the morning of the third day. He knows Blue Gums - has seen these trees before, in their native Tasmania, taller than anything. He left the afternoon of the third day, certain Blue Gums had won.

Between storms an outside breeze lifts a faint salt smell. The American leans, beer, flag in hand, other hand wraps the bar, he asks, "Which tree won?"

"The Blue Gum."

The American's face grinned, he doesn't believe that. He doesn't say so, doesn't say anything. He thinks; with Redwoods, you cannot tell the end of things, and that he, an American, in a bar they might not like Yanks in. He looks at the forest bloke who sits on a bar stool, legs bending feet to cross juts, back in a zag twist.

"I camped in Redwoods once.'

"Ones up there?"

"No, in California, camped in them with a friend.'

He and his friend had camped under those earth tapped giants; talked fearless kids talk of moon and space, (minute above the Redwoods).

They'd caught trout, it's eyes were bicycle tubes fractured through tyre skin. They'd trapped, or tried to the opossums which stole their food. A opossum caught, turned on his friend. In that good past, it clawed deeply.

"Were there possums ……. up there, in the Redwoods?"

"One, in the hut."

He'd strapped his food up in the rafters. Hung from a leather belt the possum could neither open nor attack.

"Did you make traps?"

The forest bloke nodded, no.

"Should have tried a noose trap," The American thought of that then. A wire noose with bait, they should have tried that - except his friend had the traps, his friend was clawed.

"Maybe, but they are fast."

The forest bloke drank beer, his face tight from cold and deeply tanned.

"You seen those Redwoods?"

"In California."

"They thought they would win, when they started racing everyone thought they would win."

The American says, apologetically, almost defensively, thinking you cannot tell with trees, they grow forever.

"You race everything in this country?"

"Race possums, if we could catch them."

The forest bloke laughs. The American isn't thinking of possums; but his, camped in Redwoods, talk of moon above trees and almost caught opossums, raced against Blue Gums and when lost - your past is less, moon and space greater.

The forest bloke talks possum racing, he is up to odds, he thinks it might be difficult to handicap a possum. The American finishes the stronger, Hop'ier beer, he doesn't really like. He says he'll have to leave after those two blokes he'd come in with. He says, "You haven't caught the possums to race them - you could try a noose, so long as they don't hang themselves." Like the moon, he thinks, but doesn't know why he thinks that. And leaves - not after the other blokes- but says so.

The driver stopped - a school bus, (the only transport which drove up through the hills) after a bridge in a narrow gum and myrtle valley, in a morning misted with energy. A track left the road, headed straight up the valley, "A mile up," the driver's gummed voice.

The bus rumbles gears, changing up. School kids stare from the back windows. It leaves him on a river road edge, dropping into ferns and the sound of water. A muddy track he walks up, calves aching.

He follows the track up the river valley, water thrashing down, follows it to the Redwoods.

Redwoods - he enters a moments intense recall of friend, with Redwoods, wind pitched sound, Redwoods scent and tallest on God's earth, height. He pretends that, pretends here, Redwoods are tallest, although his courage and odds will not look to see Redwoods inching passed a bluffed itself Blue Gum. He doesn't like racing, in a country where they race anything and his past is shrunk in a faint salt regret below Blue Gums which rise straight from the hills, rising sheer from an ocean. Their leaves oiled like sad, even when tallest, they are sadder than he.

An Ending

Miriam says to Nigel. "I want to hire a boat on the lake."

Miriam has been watching the boats on the lake, red and white rowboats plying in awkward directions out from the small jetty. She sits on a chair, her feet on another, her dress folded over and around her legs. Miriam has joined Nigel in Buffalo Springs to end something. Something which began two years ago and felt both like an adventure and quenched the hollowness within her, but lately only adds to the hollowness, lately, since she realized - (and not without bitterness) that he will never leave his wife, his children, his family. Of course, he won't. Maybe here, doing things they have never done before, it will have a little of the adventure at the end, it had in the beginning, maybe that will make it easier.

It had begun in a Geelong winter, rain falling from clouds black and hard, splashing across the palms in the park near the mill. Nigel works in the office, Miriam then worked on the line, a holiday job, an experience. They met in the park beneath the palms, rain running rivers along the gutters, Nigel had said, as they stood sheltering beneath the palm.

"I've seen you around."

"On the line."

Miriam then asked him if he thought it a good idea to get out of the rain. He smiled saying "Yes," he had a pleasant smile. They ran rain soaked across the park, across the road before the mill and into the office foyer where he asked if she'd have lunch in the park tomorrow if it wasn't raining. She said, she would be, and "Yes, it's okay if you join me," she didn't know then, still doesn't know now how big an "Okay," that was.

Miriam looks at Nigel sitting across the lacquered pine table in the cabin he has rented.

"We should go down to the lake where the hire boats are."

They follow the track beside the cabin which zigzags through the ironbark forest to the lake shore and around the edge of the lake to the boatman on the jetty. The boatman sits on old wooden chair tilted against the side of his hire boat shed in faded overalls and a grease stained cap, it looks as if it is a poor living hiring boats on the lake.

Miriam asks the boatman, "Do you hire boats everyday?"

"Everyday," he answers.

"If it rains?"

"Everyday includes rain."

"How much are the boats?"

"Five dollars a half hour, eight dollars an hour."

"We'll hire one for an hour tomorrow."

They continue along the track, around the lakes shore, to where the water ripples against the weir, spilling over it to renew the Springs River a deep gorge below. They sit on the rocks at the edge of the weir wall. Miriam flicks pebbles across the water, some of them skipping again and again out across the grey lake, and some splashing against the ripples a few metres from where she stands. She turns towards Nigel saying, "We should leave Geelong, we should live here in buffalo Springs and spend our lives growing apples in the hills."

Once Miriam believed those things which she says, about what she and Nigel should do, but now they have as much as anything an element of tease. Although who she is teasing she is not completely sure.

"How I wish I could do that Miriam."

Miriam kisses him lightly, knowing he cannot, and knowing a large part of her doesn't even wish it.

"I don't want you to leave your wife Nigel. I want you to leave me. I need it to finish."

Nigel doesn't say anything, he sits on the rock beneath the shadow of an oak, patches of sunlight across his face. Miriam had expected more reaction than this. She hadn't known how to say it and thought of many reactions, anger, tears, anguish, sulky? She walks along the top of the wire in the sun, ripples washing across her bare-footed toes, looking back at Nigel she thinks deceptively, how easy it is to end something.

Nigel says, "shouldn't we leave now, if this is the end."

"No," says Miriam, "I want to hire a row-boat from the boatman, I want to row far out into the lake, as far as the island and back."

I want, thinks Miriam, to snatch one more day, one last day of illusion, just one. She walks back along the broad concrete top of the weir, arms outstretched pretending to balance. When she arrives at the bank she takes Nigel's hand, dragging him from the rock saying, "Come on let's follow the track downstream to the Springs.

As they walk further along the track Miriam thinks of the beginning, of the middle and of the end. Of the first flaxen days of spring in her house at Indigo Creek, the pale muslin light of her kitchen at dusk where they cautiously revealed those inner layers of self, hesitantly their desire for each other. Later it was good to lie together in Miriam's small bed in the room which in grey daybreak overlooks the peach trees, the road running down to the wheat fields along which some time in the night Nigel had left along, leaving her to the hollowness which would creep back in with the day break. At least how she'd never have to wonder, the endless lover's question, "when will I see you again?"

"We should have tea in the Springs."

"If you like," answers a subdued Nigel.

Buffalo Springs is across a suspension bridge over the Springs River, Miriam swings the bridge as she crosses jumping from one side to the other and laughing. Laughing still at the old miner's cottages over-run with sarsaparilla vine and vast green fig trees laughing at the thought of Nigel rocking in a rocking-chair on a ramshackle verandah. They enter the Savoia Hotel, an old red brick building renovated in the fifties, the lounge bar painted pastel blue with green vinyl coated tables and a large gauche print of a Ticino Mountain scene. They sit on a table facing away from Ticino and towards the only window which looks out on a few tables under an elm, what passes as a beer garden in the Springs. Nigel asks the barmaid for a beer and a gin and lime which he carries back to the table. Nigel drinks his beer quickly. Miriam sips her gin, pushing the ice deep into the effervescent drink and watching as it revolves back to the surface.

"Do you know how to row a boat?" she asks Nigel, "I don't but I've watched couples row on the lake today and it doesn't look so difficult."

"The couples on the lake today weren't rowing anywhere except in circles and you want to row to the island."

"And I will."

Miriam goes to buy Nigel another beer from the big bussed lady in the red dress behind the bar who says to Miriam, "We don't get young people in the pub that often, maybe they can't afford beer on the dole."

"We work in a mill," says Miriam, "We can only afford one beer."

The lady smiles and tells Miriam when she was young her father was on the susso for years, he cut washing line stays in the Whipstick Forest, but no-one uses washing line stays anymore.

Miriam tells Nigel the barmaid is a good old stick who'd probably do a good counter tea, she'd ordered the trout the barmaid suggested, fresh from the lake, and it is.

They eat the trout with salad, drink another round of drinks, without saying any of the things they would have once said, about the Ticino mountain scene, the vinyl tables, like their parents used to own, or how the men across the counter in the main bar lean so lethargically in Akubra hats, talking, they suppose of rabbits and rain. Now there is only the awkward silence of each wondering, what it is like to end something.

They walk arm in arm along the twisted road which crosses the gorge and circles up to the cabin. Miriam thinking as they go, that tomorrow when they hire the boat on the lake it will be the last thing they ever do together. She tries not to think of this, not yet, she tries to live for this last night together, the last night of lying in the metallic blue light of the cabin lamp, being together in the small bed feeling warm and luscious lying together listening to the stillness of the hills. But, of course, it cannot be like this, for Nigel must ask, "Why can't we stay together, just a little longer?"

Miriam lies back against the pillows, feeling Nigel's body near and staring into the grey light of the room, "Because I don't want to."

"If I left Sharon?"

Miriam doesn't want to hear that. She doesn't want that possibility to churn around in her head again, because she knows he won't, she is certain, almost certain, he won't.

"I don't want you to, I just want it to finish tomorrow, before it becomes bitter."

"It's bitter now Miriam."

"Not that bitter."

"For me it's bitter."

They lie silently together, Nigel breathing long hurtful breaths. She has never really believed Nigel's claims of loving her, and now, if it is true, she cannot care.

Nigel says, "you must understand Miriam, sometimes it is hard, there are things which bind people together which have little to do with love, but they bind, they bind hard, and you cannot so easily tear yourself from them."

Yes, there is something which binds them together, Nigel and Sharon, it is called cowardice, and then, just then, Miriam understood, just how useless this man would be in her life. How few lakes they would row, how few islands they would explore, how few adventures they would have, just one, the island tomorrow, the day Miriam leaves Nigel and Nigel a lie.

She doesn't say that, one day he will know, she simply says, "It's over Nigel, tomorrow it has to finish, please let me go down to the boatman on the lake and hire a row-boat to take us out to the island. Just let me do that, without any bitterness, without any anger, my last day with you."

In the morning as they walk down the zigzag track to the lake, clouds gather around the hills and a light drizzle begins to fall. The boatman is dressed in the same overalls and greasy cap but with a roll neck jumper on in the cooler weather. He is sanding the bow of an unturned dingy. Miriam knocks loudly on the door of his shed.

She asks him, "Are you hiring boats today?"

He smiles at Miriam, "Everyday."

"Which boat are you hiring?"

"Any boat but this one, there is no one else going to hire a boat today."

"I want a red and white boat."

They are all red and white. Miriam sits in the oarsman's seat, Nigel in the aft. The boatman pushes them off the jetty and out into the lake. Miriam takes the oars and concentrates matching right arm with left so as not to go in circles and begins plying the small boat into the midst of the lake. The rain splashes patterns across the calm water. Nigel huddles in his jacket in the rain. Miriam rows, she doesn't care how much it rains, rain only helps keep the lake for themselves and she doesn't care if Nigel sits silently in the aft, his back against the transom, what little there is left to say she can tell him best by doing nothing but rowing.

It will end soon, they will drive separately back to Geelong, but not before she has rowed out passed the island, not until they turn into the far branch of the lake and turn back again, and not until the last hour she has brought for eight dollars is over.

Hartz River

In April, after the first autumn rain fell pumice grey in the mountains, obliterating the clear summer stream he remembered, Forest returned to the Hartz River. Thirty-five now, hair receding above a pale, vaguely veined face, bearing too much weight in the midriff and chest, he looks successful, urban. A publication officer with the Department of Education, it is the type of job his father would have nodded a waxen grey head about and said, "Steady." Forest has succeeded most in what he values least. What he values most is here at the Hartz River. This is the place where twenty years ago, for the first time he stood thigh deep in running water casting line over its surface, casting and drawing it back, casting and drawing it back and in the ease of the motion, the swift punch of the water against his legs, the cold and the calm of the eucalyptus bank, youth had a sure, exhilarating clarity.

Today he has driven from Carnegie, away from Kate, three hours to Wangaratta, turning off into the familiar countryside, the long drive up the narrowing valley to Myrtleford, skirting the Ovens River, passing tobacco fields, high-trellised hops and green grazed river flats up again to the cabin on the Hartz. Wishing as he drove, that he's walked it, as he had the first time, with khaki rucksack heavy on his back. He had felt so worthy. So, able to have taken the red clanging train out of Spencer Street by himself, to have watched adventurously, the city give way to low green hills punctuated with straight strands of pines, farmyards on long dog yapping drives and the hills beginning to rise higher and bluer to the south and east. The early train passing towns in the valleys, a few minutes in Kilmore, the red brick station, the railway hotel with thin tufts of smoke rising from a rear chimney and a lone shuffling pensioner wandering, in Bradford, in Seymour and Euroa, north then east around the high country to Myrtleford and the Hartz.

Forest jarred open the rusty iron bolt of the cabin door, opening it to find the floor littered with possum droppings, newspapers and old beer cans, to find wasp nests in the rafters and a tiny stream of water running along the floorboards from a leak in the roofing iron above the bunk. He spread a groundsheet across the upper bunk, his sleeping bag and a leather suitcase on the bunk below. The cabin will have to be cleaned before Kate arrived on Friday.

Forest followed a blackberry tangled path through the peppermint gums to the river. He walked rock to rock down the bank watching where the river washed under upturned trees, ebbing into the holes beneath. "There would be trout there, heads in the murky water, rising to grasshoppers coming down," Forest said to Forest, without conviction. "When the rain clears off the high ridges, when the clouds rise and the river subsides I will fish the Hartz again." the same Forest with the same pale green fly rod.

There was an axe that Forest found in the wood box near the fire, an old oil stone with it. He sat on a stool on the verandah sharpening the axe, rubbing the rusty metal edge, one side the another, again and again. He carried the axe across the black berried pasture to the bush beyond. He was clumsy and weak. The axe rebounded off the hardest red box with barely a scratch cut. He cut what he could, mostly the old rotting timber lying in the understory of the bush and carried it back to the cabin.

He lit the fire, billy beside it, beans and eggs in the frying pan. It felt good, as it did the first time after the hard walk from Myrtleford; he had arrived footsore, calves aching, yet with youth's insuppressible energy, he had chopped a couple of days worth of wood, cooked rice and salami and in the lingering summer evening, gone down to the river to learn to cast fly-line inelegantly across the water.

He had cracked the fly-line too hard, whipping the flies into the trees on the bank. He tempered his action and found that the flies fell somewhere near where he wanted, the line returned mostly without tangling and the next cast flowed more surely than the last. It pleased him and gave him courage although he caught no trout.

Over that summer he fished the Rose River, the Buffalo, and the Dandongadale but came back always to the Hartz. He caught a few trout, walked many miles along the logging tracks, camped in the solitary places where a person will talk to a person he meets. Here Forest met the trampers who pointed out the small things he missed; the way the trees changed as you rose up the spurs, where the snow lay longest in the southern gullies and how to read a stream by the trees and the insects on the bank. They taught Forest; how to pack his rucksack, tight and small, to walk very lightly and steadily and to read, instead of map and compass, the way the hills formed, the rivers flowed and the vegetation changed, in fact, to see and note everything.

These things became Forest's first small truths, the first things which weighed on his memory and were his.

A twilight on the Mount Cobbler Plateau beside the darkening west bank of the lake with the distant sunlit east bank turning the same golden grey as the eucalyptus above. Here a poet, who'd once lived in San Guiraud, France, had told Forest he should use the things he had discovered, should write it all down, for although, the discipline of art is lonely and demanding for those who see clearly, there is no other way. The day he climbed the Hewitt Spur in driving sleet, to rise above the clouds at the summit and see Victoria tumble below him. The day he fished the Hartz, the water a faultless clarity and the trout hanging kites within it.

He began to write his story of the mountains, but discovered as he tried to write, how difficult it is, for everything he began failed to say what he wanted to say. Yet he knew, he would write eventually, it was the one thing he never doubted.

Forest woke in the first light, a red smudge of sun behind the eastern ridges, the sky deep mauve and clear. He split wood on the stones beside the fireplace, began a small fire, boiling water for tea and to wash in, frying eggs and toasting bread. Forest washed naked on the verandah, vapour rose from the bowl, delicate whiffs from his body. He splashed water from the white enamel bowl across his face, the back of his neck and his chest, the water lukewarm, the air lacquered with frost. He dressed hurriedly. Forest swept cobwebs from the rafters, possum droppings from the cupboard tops and the floor. He swept and mopped, scrubbed the large wooden table and moved it under the window which overlooked the river, placing books and writing pad on it, the best chair in the cabin beside. He made a cup of tea on his old "trange" and sat sipping it on the desk.

Forest had not become the writer he dreamt of becoming, and his desk in the cabin on the Hartz River was no more than a ritual. He felt vaguely foolish to have clung to this dream; except there had never been anything since which had filled him with so much worth. He clung on, sitting on the desk, trying once more to write. On this day, he wrote no more than "Hartz River 91". It wasn't a bad sign. The only original story Forest had ever published, he had only written "Paris October 81" the first day, that first exhilarating day in the great city. It was too long ago now, but those first weeks there, seemingly fulfilling his youthful ambition, still filled him with warmth.

From the Cherbourg ferry, a low coastline under frayed cloud had looked like the coast across the heads from Point Lonsdale, except that it felt immensely significant to step onto the quay below the grey slate buildings of Northern France. to buy a ticket to Paris at the Cherbourg station, to travel from Normandy in a second-class compartment full of National Service soldiers, the long fields and woods outside. Forest had sat next to Kate, thinking that at the end of this journey he would write in the city which made writers; if he couldn't write here, he couldn't write anywhere. He had stood against the doorway watching the suburbs of Paris as the Cherbourg train drew into the Gare St. Lazare, afraid.

They had found a hotel off the Rue Lacepede and a cafe on the Rue de Navarre where Forest had sat drinking "une demi" of beer, a journalist's spiral notebook beside him. That day he had only written "Paris October 81", and because the city was so new he had gone with Kate to see the Seine, the ill St. Louis, where at another cafe Forest had told Kate that he already knew this city would help him write.

In the morning, he had written again in the cafe, ordering coffee and trying to find the words that told how it was on the track beyond Bennies, the Rose River running swiftly from Mount St. Bernard obscured in mist. He had wanted it to have the feeling of Ernest Hemingway's "Two Hearted River," to take you into the land and the river of his youth. He has begun from the Rose River bridge, watching the Parisians on the street, he had written, "Along the grey gravel road the pine trees grew...." Later Kate had come down from the hotel to share a coffee and Forest had told her how fine it felt. "Fine," was a word Ernest Hemingway used continually; he'd probably used it one rain-washed December of 21 when Hadley would have come down from the hotel Jacob to share a coffee. He was writing "Up in Michigan" then. It had still felt fine then. He didn't know then that everything had already been destroyed, for Hemingway or Forest, he wasn't sure.

Forest sat at the desk for an hour. And later he went onto the verandah to re-sharpen the axe, looking at the trees at the edge of the bushland; a great and ancient forest of trees began here and grew unbroken from range to range to the farmlands skirting the southern coast. He threw his axe into the hard core of a fallen tree. It shuddered, splitting large chips of wood into the air. He lifted and swung, again and again, turning the log with his boot as he cut. He sweated heavily. He would need a large wood stack before the weekend when Kate would drive up from Carnegie. She didn't like the cold and would think the Hartz river cabin too primitive. If he had enough firewood it might be better.

Forest was reluctant to burn too much of his split wood that night. He found some wood on the riverbank which burnt insipidly and cooked his curry slowly. He made the curry very hot for himself, too hot for Kate. It was a calm, cold night and Forest couldn't sleep in the unaccustomed stillness. He thought how he would write in the morning, how he thought so long ago, the first time on the Hartz, that he would accomplish so much. And he thought, without Kate beside him, of the bitterness which separated them.

They lived on the Barwon River estuary where it swept around the marshy lowlands in the west up against the low orchard hills of the Bellarine Peninsula. Their house on the estuary edge, a small green fibre house nestled in the tee-tree heath, from it you could see over the estuary to the bridge at the heads and further to the straight where squalls swept in, dark, intense, threatening. She was unknown to him, slender with long thin hair tied behind her back, in faded jeans and sandals she sat beside him on the banks of the estuary. In clear light, they spoke the talk of youth, of improbable ambition, to write, full of yearnings and the bitter, true, things of life, to live in a place like this, beside the slow flowing

Barwon by mud flat and heath bank on the precarious income of writing. She shared Forest's dreams, or seemed to, and soon afterwards shared the small bed in the enclosed verandah coming in red nightshirt to love and talk, lying close in the pale glow of Skinner's Caltex sign on the corner. When that closeness vanished, when the first intensity subsided, that was harsh enough, but later in St. Felix de Sorgues in the white room with the grey shutters, overlooking the village place, he discovered that Kate had been lost to him. In the year before France, when he cared only for his great expatriate dream, while he worked night shifts at Costas packing vegetables, she had spent time with an art teacher, who'd flattered her, challenged her, and, yes, slept with her. But what, she asked, did he care, so obsessed was he with the craziness of writing, which locked her out, locked everything out.

"You're still locking me out," she had screamed, hurling a bottle of Moulin-a-Vent against the stone stairway.

It was true, remained true, but now Forest did it with a spitefulness, daring her to find another, to leave him to his obsession.

Is that what Forest truly wanted? He couldn't answer that, that evening with the Midi heat still radiating off the stone-walled vineyards, Forest had walked to the cafe at St. Paul. Subdued and a little drunk, he'd come back along the Sorgues River road where below the olive groves and Sulphur splattered vineyards, he had found a kitten in the gutter. What an absurd offering! A Midi kitten in the night.

In the stunning frost chill of dawn, Forest began to write. In the publications branch and as a journalist before that, he has written ceaselessly, about dill pickles, car accidents, flower shows, the history of Clunes, about everything and anything, except about Forest. To write the truth about Forest was what he found difficult and, if he was honest, a little frightening, to see within, to enunciate and to know.

He wanted to write it all down, and he wanted it to be true. He thought about beginnings, his birth, his earliest memory, he sitting in his grandmother's garden in Nedlands, Forest sitting in what must have been a high chair, he wasn't sure, for what impinged on his memory wasn't the chair, or himself but the lucidity of the light through the oaks. He wrote number one in his notebook, underlined it, then wrote, "I remember a kind of pale green, like the inside of an Iceberg lettuce," but as always, this wasn't how he knew it to be.

He tore that sheet of paper off his pad and placed it in a plastic folder, wrote number two, and underlined it. He tried to think of that first time walking up from Myrtleford, the birth of his independence. He'd hitch-hiked up from Wangaratta in early morning, dumped his rucksack in the back of an old green E.H. Holden ute, driven by a timber worker, who'd dropped him at the old Myrtleford train station, the sun entering beyond the station eves lighting the brown metal benches, carnations flowering pink in terracotta pots and a long exact line of light ducking under the Myrtleford sign. It was warm in the sun when he left the ute and timber worker, warm while he checked the pockets of his rucksack, checked his map and the directions his grandfather had written to the old fishing cabin on the Hartz. "It ain't much, don't get used much no more, but it's ours." He felt for the first time the lingering crisp air of the mountains, that unforgettable air which he would always associate with, early summer dawn waste deep in the Hartz, casting fifteen metres of faint, air hanging line, over the water.

There is another cold of the Hartz. It is still and close and breathes caustic in the nostrils, it is the cold of snow on Mount Typo, on Warrick, on Mount Emu. on the Cobbler plateau, and Forest had never smelt to as intently as he did today.

This was the smell of blizzards.

Forest watched the clouds obscure the ridges. He thought of Kate. She hated cold and would arrive unprepared for this. He would spend the afternoon again cutting wood. It was good to sweat the flabby mid-dle-aged body, good to fill the afternoon. Today it would be very cold, sleet mist would soak under coat and cap and run miserably wet into his jumper, shirt and into his skin, when he finished trying to write, he would split wood for Kate.

Early winter snow fell on the higher ridges. It came in massive cumulus squalls leaving ragged cloud ebbies in gullies and cols. This was the day Kate would come to the Hartz River and Forest spent it preparing for her, cleaning floors and benches, sealing windows and roof, building a fire early so it would be warm enough when she came, and preparing his thoughts.

The years since their return from France had been marred by bitterness, by Forest's failure to fulfil his ambition, and by a steady draining domesticity. He knew, he guessed Kate also knew, that his coming back to the Hartz was an undefined separation. Forest didn't know how it would be with Kate when she arrived. Kate didn't know how it would be with Forest when she arrived, neither Kate nor Forest knew, how they would like it to be.

She left early in the afternoon, not realizing how far it is to the Hartz River, driving over range after range into the east of Victoria. She said, when she arrived, "It's bloody miles, it's bloody freezing!" Forest showed Kate a chair near the fire he'd been burning since mid afternoon. It was glowing with red coals, a giant split slab of red box perched above. He had a billy on a rock in the coals from which he poured boiling water, making Kate and himself a mug of fresh ground coffee. She didn't say anything while she sat, warmed by the fire, sipping her coffee. She glanced around.

"It's not much of a cabin."

"It's not too bad."

"This is where you came when you were young?"

"Yes, the last time the summer before I met you."

Kate remembered the intense conversations about the Hartz River. Forest was in love with this place, and something of it's wildness, it's mystery, was within him. It was attractive then. Kate wondered why she had never been to the cabin before, of course, she would have and did detest it, it's bareness, it's primitiveness and the dark squalls of rain, mist and flurries of sleet.

They ate the less-hot curry that Forest had cooked, plates on their laps near the fire. Forest turned the radio to the ABC. The sound crackled, faded and returned as storms on the ridges blasted the high country.

"It's snowing." said Forest.

"Where?"

"All around us."

"Will it snow here?"

"We are probably too low."

"But it could?"

"I suppose so, if it got cold enough."

"It's got to be cold enough now."

Forest lit a lamp and he and Kate got into the small bunk listening to the radio. Years ago, thought Forest, in the verandah room on the estuary they might have made love and lain afterwards in the warm sweaty closeness, laughing at the crackling, inaudible "Goon Show'. They lay instead apart in the small bed and slept fitfully.

At dawn the clouds had parted, a frosty mist had fallen piercingly cold along the Hartz. Forest lit the fire from the overnight coals, boiling coffee and washing water. Kate woke, drew the sleeping bag around herself and said, "It's snow cold." Forest handed her a cup of coffee which they sat silently drinking.

"You have to wash with the water in the hand bowl."

"You're joking."

"No."

She watched Forest wash quickly beside the low morning fire, then followed him, splashing water quickly over her face and body. She was no longer as slight as she'd been in the house on the Barwon, but the little extra weight looked good on her. They dressed in jackets and boots laced up over ankles and went down to the Hartz River flowing from mist choked pool quick and glassy into lower mist choked pool. Kate sat on a boulder by the banks.

"I have been trying to write again."

"Is that good?"

"It hasn't gone well, I haven't got it clear in my mind."

Kate looked at Forest squatting on a low boulder, the water swirling at it's edge, a clear, constant ebbie which glides beneath his boots. Kate feared that, feared the return to the Hartz for that reason. Here, the dream of his youth was too intimate. Here, if it fails, and it has always failed, it will be so much more devastating. She also realized, it may as well be now, and she supposed Forest also knew, it may as well be now.

She asked, smiling bleakly, "Is there trout in there?"

"There are some in the top pool," He said glancing upstream to where the mist was rising in long tapering strands into the blackwood boughs, "but there is better fishing downstream at the flats, I'll show you the flats."

"Yes," says Kate.

They walked rock to rock down the rapids then up on the bank passed the deep lower hole. Tee-tree and blackberry forced them away from the bank, and they had to brush their way through the dense foliage to come back again to the river. It was damp and very cold, pale sunlight hit the far bank but this side of the river was in frozen shadow until they came out at the flats. There the bank opened up into small grassy meadows, the river a long sweeping eddy of water between them.

"It's hard to believe I last fished this river twenty one years ago."

Kate unbuttoned her jacket and lay it on the ground; she sat on it in the slight warmth of the sun, looking at the paunchy, balding Forest, finding it not so hard to believe. The ground smelt damp and muddy, the air a eucalyptus fragrant; she could have almost dozed except Forest came and sat beside her.

He didn't say anything; he had locked her out again. Kate began to regret coming up here to Forest's Hartz River, there are other things she could be doing, other people she could be with.

They walked back along the track. It rose above the river along a low north-western spur, twisting upwards and down again to the Hartz River bridge near the cabin. It was a hard climb. They stopped at the highest point, Kate's calves aching. She looked at the ridges falling away, dusted white with snow she had never seen before.

"I'd like to touch it," she said.

"It will be gone this afternoon. It's only the first fall and it will be too warm on the ridges for it to last long."

"It's a shame."

Kate squatted against a fallen tree, resting for a minute before the track down, which was as steep as it was up.

At the cabin Kate was calf weary and blistered. She took boots and socks off, aired her feet in the sun. Forest made tea and sandwiches which he brought out to her on the verandah, then went back into the cabin and brought out his rod, reel, and flies. He opened the small can he kept his flies in, a lozenge can he'd brought in St. Paul, and looked at the delicate feathered flies. He liked the flies, he liked the way they looked, like Klee might have drawn a cricket or a fingerling, and he liked the memories they revived. The Sorges River road below the long limestone escarpment, stone closed vineyards parched bluey-yellow with Bordeaux mix, stepped in tiers up to the escarpment and cypresses along the road. Monsieur Vevy in customary blue jacket fished with a long French cane pole, flicking it metres ahead over the glint water, while Forest fished like an Englishman, with fly line and leader. Monsieur Vevy caught trout; Forest didn't.

Forest took his reel apart, cleaned and oiled it, then threaded the line through the rod.

"Are you coming to the river?"

"No, I'll sit here in the sun."

Forest walked down the track to the river, stopping when he reached it's banks to watch the water, to sense where the trout might lie, flicking silver bodies into the flow. He chose a wet mud-eye, tied it to his line and moved quietly into the knee-high waters, slowly feeding his line out as he moved up the river. He landed his line well, brought it back cleanly and landed it again softly on the water. It felt good, just to watch it come down on the surging water, to feel it grip ever so delicately on the epidermis of the river. It was enough. He moved through the holes, the water waist deep and cold, back into the running water, working his line hard. In a knee-deep slide of water, he felt his line grab. Trout, it swished at the surface then dived. Forest moved forward bringing the line in, then cautiously drew the fish up, it threshed, zig-zagging across the Hartz as Forest drew it closer, closer, with rod bowed into his net. He was happy. It was a good river. He was glad Kate was here.

They cooked trout on the fire Kate had lit in the cabin, ate it with potatoes she had cooked in the coals, tomato and capsicums. They built up the fire again and sat beside it for a while in the night, the radio on, rain beginning to speckle across the tin roofed cabin. They sat slightly apart from each other the Tilley lamp acting larger than life shadows on the stone fireplace.

"In the morning, I'll fish again."

"Yes," said Kate.

Her face was in the shadow of the lamp and lit only by the flames, a coarse but vibrant light.

"I'll leave after lunch."

They listened to the radio, Forest wishing he could tell Kate he was glad she was here, but they didn't say things like that to each other any more. He felt a sadness, like looking within him through the wrong end of a telescope at that pure intensity of love they once shared.

In the morning, he didn't wake Kate but went alone to the river with rod and flies. He cast line again, moving slowly upstream. This morning he didn't catch anything and he returned disappointed to the cabin to start a morning fire, make coffee and toast and boil some washing water. Kate was awake.

They drank the coffee. Forest on the bed next to Kate handing her pieces of toast.

"It'll be lonely here," she said.

"I'll be alright."

"What will you do?"

"Write."

Before she left they walked across the split log bridge over the Hartz and along the upstream track. It followed close to the river and was an easy walk. They walked quietly, Forest occasionally pointing out to Kate the good holes of the river. They startled wallabies grazing the meadows near the bank, and then they and she were gone. Forest spent the rest of that Sunday splitting box wood to clear his mind.

The next morning the cabin was engulfed in cloud. Forest sat at his table only seeing a few metres of verandah beyond the window. He could not write. He could only wonder how we can be so many different people to each other. He thought of the autumn of 71, the first year, the French autumn of 81 and within that decade how dreams had soured.

It could have worked; if he'd written the story of his brother and him, Neil Marriott, and his sister driving across the peninsula, along Main Ridge road to the sea, Neil with fine fish net held atop the Morris Minor convertible, the wind whistling through, the sea distant, but each twist of road into green myrtle gullies and up onto farmland raking hay in the warm December brought it closer, so now you could see it, a thin far blue line, a little latter a wave break, distant on reefs, then a strip of coast to the east, fishing boats, a beach below, and the pale rocks around the cape to Flinders. If he could have written it with the feeling of youth awakening to the tug of the sea. And if he could have written of the days at Barwon Heads, the first time on the Hartz, the night of the kitten at St. Felix de Sorgues. If he had written it down well, and his dreams had not soured, that part of himself that he most cherished, may not have closed in on itself, closed to Kate and the bitterness may not have begun.

Forest didn't know if the bitterness was not inescapable. He went out of the cabin and sat on the verandah. The mist was thickening, the morning colder. He sat on the seat where Kate had sat and looked into the place where the trees should begin somewhere in the mist, and Forest began to feel the deep loneliness of the Hartz.

He dragged on his ankle length walking boots and put on his oil skin coat. He went out into the mist to walk up the track, over the ridge and down to the flats again. To go again to the grassy banks of the Hartz where Kate had put down her coat to sit there again beside where she would have lain, to coax from his mind what he wanted to say, what he needed to say then, but couldn't.

He couldn't then, even to the vacant banks of the Hartz River, he couldn't.

Forest returned to the cabin. Mud washed down the track, soaking boots, socks, dungarees, sleet dripped inside his oil-skin coat. Very wearily he climbed up to the height of the spur where snow fell exhausted.

Absolute autumn snow, fell absolutely still.

Forest hesitated, thinking, if only.

If only Kate would return to the cabin next Friday, to the disintegrating marriage, to him.

If only he could write, "Snow fell," with the same absolute clarity. Defying his expectations, he did.

It began a love story.

Acknowledgements

Memoirs of a Binocular'd girl has been previously published in *Island in the Sun*, Sea Cruise Books, 1981; *Atelier du Gue*, Breves, Villelongue d'Aude, France, 1982

The Bay of Islands has been previously published in *Riverrun*, Newcastle 1976: *The State of the Art*, Ed. Frank Moorhouse, Penguin Books 1983; *Morning Parrot Trees*, Red Press Sydney 1979.

In a house of Geckos has been previously published in *Compass*, Sydney, 1979; *Morning Parrot Trees*.

The Master of the Melancholy Carp has been previously published in *Morning Parrot Trees*.

The Want Buyer and Crocodile Eye has been previously published in *Morning Parrot Trees*.

The Osprey of Fatty George has been previously published in *Atelier du Gue* Breves, Villelongue d'Aude, France, 1985

The Fisherman and a dragon Atoll has been previously published in *Morning Parrot Trees*.

The Desert of Khan Mahomed has been previously published in *Morning Parrot Trees*.

Morning Parrot Trees has been previously published in *Compass*, Sydney, 1980 ; *Morning Parrot Trees*.

Possum Moon and Redwoods has been previously published in *Inprint*, the Short Story Magazine, Sydney, 1978 ; *Australian Mag.* Sydney, 1981, *Morning Parrot Trees*.

Hartz River has been previously published in *Fictions 88,* A.B.C. Books, Sydney, 1988.

www.ingramcontent.com/pod-product-compliance
Lightning Source LLC
Chambersburg PA
CBHW020702030726
47498CB00002B/604